ASHES

BURNING MOON SERIES NOVELLA

RK CLOSE

BIG TREE

PUBLISHING

ALSO BY RK CLOSE

Vampire Files Trilogy

Red Night

Red Moon

Red Dream

Madness

Redemption - 2023

Burning Moon Series

Spark

Ignite

Blaze

Ashes

Better Off Dead - 2022

CHAPTER
ONE

THE LAST OF the dinner crowd had emptied out about twenty minutes earlier, leaving Harmony and me to clean up and close. I didn't mind the work since I got to spend time with her. The *Greasy Spoon* wasn't the most romantic setting, but after dating for four years, we were comfortable with one another in most situations.

"Please take this out back before it explodes," Harmony said, pointing at the garbage bin in the kitchen. I'd been working at the diner for over two years, but Harmony only started last summer. We worked so well together, the owner, Mrs. Bueller trusted us to close the restaurant on our own.

Grinning, I walked toward her. Instead of grabbing the bag of garbage, I slipped my arms around her waist and pulled her against me. Harmony had always felt like a perfect fit in my arms. "How about I take you to the storage room for a break? I missed mine during the rush." I nuzzled her neck.

"Liam McKenzie! You are impossible. Let me go so I can finish. I promised Lisa I'd come right over after work," she said, making a half-hearted effort to get away from me.

"Why does Lisa get all of your attention these days?" I asked, finally letting her slip out of my grasp.

Harmony put her hands on her hips and gave me that look—the one that said I wasn't being nice.

"She's having a crisis and needs to talk. I'm spending the night at her place." She picked up the rag she'd been using and began wiping down the stainless-steel counters in the kitchen.

"Lisa is always having a crisis. What's wrong now?" I asked while pulling the garbage bag out of the container.

Last month it was her weight, even though a strong wind could have knocked that girl over. Lisa was convinced she was five pounds too heavy and therefore, the world was coming to an end.

"Robert broke up with her over a text message. Can you believe that? They've been dating for almost two years. She's pretty hurt by it and I don't blame her." She had moved on to wiping down tables and then placing chairs on top of them so we could sweep and mop. That was usually the last thing we did.

"Well, he's in college and living a thousand miles away. It makes it hard to have a relationship." I walked toward the back door with the garbage in hand. When she didn't respond, I stopped to look at her. She was watching me with an odd expression I couldn't read. "What?"

"It's nothing. We'll talk more when you finish

with the trash." I thought I saw a flash of sadness in her eyes before she covered it with a brief smile. Something tightened in my gut, but I did what she asked, without pressing her further.

The alley had one light shining down over the steps from the diner. Its usefulness was almost nonexistent by the time it reached the dumpster across the alley.

I tossed the bag of trash into the large metal bin, which made a loud thumping noise as it hit bottom. A high-pitched squeal came from the shadows and my heart leaped into my throat.

"Who's there?" I called.

A familiar voice responded, "Go back inside, Liam. You scared Renee." A female voice giggled from the other side of the alley, where I could barely make out two forms sitting on the tailgate of a truck—*my truck.*

It was old, beat up, and had been ridden hard, but it was paid for and it was mine.

"Seth! What are you doing in the alley?" I asked. "I need a ride home, by the way. Harmony has plans that don't include me." Seth's car had a nail in the tire, and instead of having it fixed before the tire store closed, he asked to borrow my truck while I was working.

Renee laughed nervously again. She was only a junior in high school, so I tried not to let her voice annoy me.

Seth had his arm around her, and I wondered if she knew her shirt was still hiked up over her bra. At least I hoped that was her bra.

"We're having a chat about…" He looked at Renee, noticed her shirt, and casually pulled it down. "…life and the meaning of it all." This sent Renee into more fits of laughter that made me want to cringe.

Seth's charming grin was only one of the many things that got my younger brother into trouble on a regular basis. I didn't need to see his smile to know it was there.

"Take Renee home and come back for me. We'll be finished in a few minutes." I turned away and started walking back to the diner.

"You're always spoiling the fun, Liam," Seth called.

Down the alley, I could see Main Street, which was lit far better than the alley. From my vantage point, I could see the local bar across the road with its colorful neon signs glowing in the windows. A row of shiny polished motorcycles was parked next to the curb.

"And Renee, didn't your mama teach you to stay away from guys like Seth?" The gray metal door closed behind me, thankfully, cutting off Renee's laughter.

I heard voices in the restaurant when there shouldn't have been since the diner was now closed.

Damn it. I'd forgotten to turn the sign and lock the door. I quickly made my way to the front.

Harmony was speaking to three men dressed in leather and covered in ink. "I told you, we're closed," Harmony said, annoyed.

Knowing her, they must have said or done something to upset her. Harmony had a great way with everyone, even the grumpiest of customers. When I walked in, the bikers and Harmony turned to look at me.

"What seems to be the problem?" I asked.

"I've told these *gentlemen* that the diner is closed, but they insist on being served." Harmony's words were firm, but I could see the concern in her eyes.

The shorter man in the group stepped forward and studied me openly. His expression seemed almost curious and maybe surprised.

Did they believe Harmony was alone?

"The sign says open, and the door was unlocked. That says *welcome* to me." He nodded his head at the door behind him. His body language suggested that he was the leader of these two, at least.

The man was thick and muscular with dark, messy hair that reached his shoulders. I was certain I could take him—not sure I could handle three at once, though. I hoped the situation wouldn't turn ugly.

"She's right. We're closed. The kitchen isn't serving any more food. Sorry about the confusion with the sign. That was my mistake. Doors open at six tomorrow for breakfast if you're interested." I kept my tone friendly, but my expression left no room for discussion as I moved to stand between Harmony and the men.

The leader eyed me up and down, taking my measure no doubt, while the other two shuffled position a bit, seeming more alert than before. I took notice of them, but my gaze never left the man doing the talking.

"What pack you with?" he asked me.

I glanced back at Harmony and she shrugged her shoulders.

"I don't know what you're talking about." His expression turned steely and for a second his eyes appeared to glow. I blinked, and they were the same dark color again.

Almost instantly, my stomach began cramping and perspiration broke out over my body as if I'd suddenly started a fever. Couldn't have been worse timing.

As if noticing my discomfort, the man smiled slowly before laughing outright. The other two began chuckling as well. "A rogue, then. Tell you what, instead of killing you, I'll make you a deal you can't refuse."

Harmony gasped. The hair on the back of my neck stood on end and my heart pounded loud enough I was sure everyone in the room could hear it.

I backed up until I felt Harmony place her hands on my shoulders. "What are you talking about? You need to leave now or I'm calling the sheriff," I said.

My greatest concern was keeping Harmony safe.

"Lone wolves aren't allowed, kid. Join our pack and all is forgiven. You'll be protected." When I looked at him in confusion, he added, "This is a generous offer. You should take it while you still can."

At that moment the bell chimed as Seth sauntered into the diner. All three men turned to look at him. One guy made a noise that sounded like a growl. Once again, my stomach turned and began cramping.

What the hell did I eat?

Seth sauntered in like he owned the place, smiling at everyone without prejudice. I couldn't tell if he picked up on the tension in the atmosphere or not. Seth was smart, almost too smart for his own good. He hid it well with plenty of bad behavior and habits.

"Liam, what's taking you so long? Pa and Cole are waiting in the truck. Let's go, let's go!" Seth claps his hands several times as if his enthusiasm would make it happen. Now I knew his game. Pa and Cole were at home.

The leader turned to me and glared. "I'll be seeing you around, *Liam*," he said before turning to leave. He stopped at the door to glare at Seth. Of course, Seth had no fear of anyone or anything. He was born with a few screws loose.

Seth gave the man one of his wide cheesy grins and waved bye as the bikers went through the door. If looks could kill, my brother would be dead three times over.

As soon as the door closed behind them, I hurried to lock it and turn the sign. I stood there and watched them walk across the street and noticed there were seven motorcycles in total. They had friends.

My sudden flu-like symptoms seemed to have left with the bikers. I'd never believed myself a coward, but my body's physical reaction to the threat suggested otherwise.

Disappointed in myself, I turned back to look at Harmony, who was as white as a sheet. She held her cell phone tightly in her hand, like a weapon.

"I've already called the sheriff."

Seth groaned loudly. "Damn, Harmony. Now we'll be here all night. Can you cancel them?"

Harmony looked at Seth like he was insane. Tears filled her eyes and she turned away before they could fall. I glared at Seth before hurrying to her. "You weren't here, Seth. They threatened to kill us," I added over my shoulder.

"Those losers? They couldn't find their asses, much less do any real damage. I'm sure they were bluffing—trying to intimidate is all. You know they're not from around here. Just passing through, no doubt." Seth sat in one of the booths and began scrolling through his phone.

Yep, loose screws.

When I turned Harmony around she'd already dried her eyes on her sleeve. "Hey. It's okay. They're gone, and you're safe."

She pulled out of my arms. "Liam, they wanted to kill you. Did you hear what they said? They were talking crazy! I was so afraid they'd hurt you."

"They were high on something. I couldn't make sense of what he was blabbering about. I was busy trying to figure out how to keep you safe. Not being sure that I could was the worst feeling I've ever felt." I pulled her to me then and she let me. We held each other tightly.

A few minutes passed, then we heard a siren getting closer. I looked over at Seth, who rolled his eyes before returning to his preoccupation with his phone. When I looked out the window again, the motorcycles were gone—*for good, I hoped.*

CHAPTER
TWO

My body feels like it's on fire. *Staring up at the full moon, I instinctively know that there's something significant about it, but the reason escapes me.*

I recognize the woods that skirt the eastern border of our territory. The air is cool, but I don't mind the temperature.

I'm confused. Why am I here?

The question is quickly forgotten when a distinct scent catches my attention. Suddenly, I'm running for the trees. I don't slow or stop as I enter the thick tangle of foliage, careless of the branches that snag my skin and tear at my flesh.

Nothing matters but finding my prey. I'm fleetingly aware of my speed, faster than I've ever been able to run. The feeling is exhilarating and terrifying at the same time. It's as if there were two of me. One, free from fear and thrilled by the hunt— the other, fearful of the need that's begun to consume me.

With every step, the old me is disappearing, like a disguise, I've worn for too long. I run and run. Time is lost to the new me. The smells of the forest are so much more complex than I'd ever realized. But one scent floating on the air and growing ever stronger is the only one that matters. I'm so close to what I seek.

And then I see it.

A bonfire in the clearing lights up a small field and casts elongated shadows of the humans standing around the flames.

Humans?

My desire to kill is instinctual. As I clear the forest and enter the field, pain rips through my body like none I've ever felt before. There is a moment when I believe the pain will rip me in half. Still, I don't break my speed. I push through it, toward it.

One of the humans turns, noticing my approach. He growls, alerting the others, but I'm only concerned with the one, the alpha. When he looks in my direction, I recognize the leader from another dream—another life. His expression isn't as confident this time. There's a challenge in his glowing amber eyes, but also a hint of fear.

That's what I feed off when I launch myself into the night. When I land, I'm closer to the ground and running the last few yards on four legs instead of two. The pain that gripped me a moment ago is no more.

So much freedom.

Leaping one last time, I land on the leader, hitting him in the chest with my full weight, knocking him off balance and driving him to the ground. My jaws are powerful when I bite into the arm he holds up to defend himself. The others step back but don't interfere. I have no fear of them. They won't do anything unless I lose this battle.

A faint voice in the darkest corners of my mind wonders how I know these things. But that voice grows more silent with every heartbeat. When I finally taste blood in my mouth, the feeling is close to euphoria. It's as though I was given a dose of adrenaline. My teeth rip and tear at the arm until I sense a change in my enemy.

His arm in my mouth seems to soften and shift. I'm startled momentarily, and my enemy takes advantage by kicking me off with powerful legs. I roll several times, trying to right myself. By the time I'm standing again, a great black wolf stands where my enemy was.

But, he is my enemy.

We circle each other, growling, teeth gnashing, jaws snapping in warning. The others circle us but I only focus on him. He has threatened my family, my pack. There are no morals, no choices, no sense of conscience. If he lives, we die.

Without warning my enemy lunges at me. I don't cower or shy away. Instead, I meet him in the air. When we collide, with a stroke of luck, I locked down hard on his throat with my jaws. I don't dare let go. He thrashes and flails.

I hear growls and even cries from the others. With a viciousness born of survival, I jerked my *head back and forth until blood suddenly floods my mouth.*

One final jerk and the large black wolf lay still. I continue to ravage my enemy, while faintly aware the others were backing away—leaving me to my kill.

I growl and snap warnings to them until one by one they disappear into the forest. When they're gone, I look around. The dark tree line surrounding the field seems larger than before. I scan the trees and the deeper parts of the forest beyond. Finally, I look down at the dead man before me. Gone is the great wolf.

That small voice returns with a vengeance, screaming, 'What have you done?'

The phone lying next to the bed was blaring an obnoxious ringtone. I reached to silence it before my ears began to bleed.

Sunlight streamed into the bedroom, adding to the nauseous feeling I'd had since waking. My head was pounding so badly I thought it must be a migraine.

Normally a morning person, I couldn't bring myself to get out of bed. Every fiber in my body was on fire. Something wasn't right. I had no time to be sick.

There was too much that needed to be done. A farm wasn't something you could clock in and out of. There were chores that had to be done, animals that depended on us, and everyone had their own jobs to do.

Knowing what I had to do didn't make it any easier. It was all I could do to drag my aching body from the bed. I sat on the edge and waited for the pounding to ease just enough. It didn't.

I reached for a pair of faded and torn jeans laying over a wooden chair next to the bed. Those jeans weren't purchased in a fashion store. They were faded and worn from hard wear and tear.

Cole used to joke about selling his old work jeans for big money on *eBay*. I wouldn't be surprised if he had. That kid always had cash and no job.

Pulling the jeans on, I decided to forgo the t-shirt. My skin was damp from that small effort.

I made my way to the bathroom down the hall and splashed water on my face. While looking in the mirror, the dream came creeping into my thoughts. I clutched the sink for support as the images came back to me as clear as day.

Though I'd been having bad dreams over the last couple of months, this was the most vivid dream I could recall. The thought of what I did and how I did it made my stomach heave. Whatever was left after dinner the night before came up violently, and I barely made it to the toilet.

After cleaning myself up, I felt better but not great. Walking down the creaking stairs of the old farmhouse, I touched the picture of Molly as I went. My way of saying good morning to the woman I called Mama for as long as I could remember. I'd been touching that same picture of my adopted mother for a year—ever since she passed away.

Her portrait hung in the middle of many other family photos, most of my two brothers and me.

Molly loved her photos almost as much as she loved us.

I moved slower than normal down the stairs, each step heavier than the last. If Mama had been there, she'd have insisted I go back to bed, and would have made chicken soup. She would have checked on me each hour, dabbing my face with a cool damp cloth. Molly was so loving and kind. It was almost worth getting sick to have her dote on us like that. We all missed her something awful.

Before I hit the bottom of the stairs, Cole came from behind, skipping the last few steps. He practically knocked me over as he barely avoided a collision with the front door, carried by his momentum.

"Morning, Liam," he said without looking at me.

"Nothing good about it," I muttered under my breath.

I turned the corner into the kitchen, the smell of bacon floated on the air. Ordinarily, breakfast with the family was my favorite way to start the day. That morning, the smell and thought of food made my stomach feel queasy again.

When I entered the kitchen, Pa was sitting at the table reading the paper with a steaming cup of coffee next to him. Seth was at the stove preparing eggs, bacon, and hash browns...none of which sounded appetizing.

"Glad you decided to grace us with your presence, big brother," Seth said over his shoulder.

Pa never looked up from his paper but asked,

"I heard you had some trouble at the diner last night. Anything you need to tell me?"

"Something happened at the diner last night? Why am I always the last to hear the good stuff?" Cole asked with too much interest to be healthy.

Pa gave him that fatherly look but said nothing.

"Someone has to be last, Cole. Just accept your fate, boy," Seth teased.

Cole rolled his eyes. His sandy blond hair was cut short on the sides and longer on top so that some of it always hung over one of his eyes. He was constantly pulling it back, which he did then. Pa was always threatening to cut it off for him.

"How'd you know?" Seth asked while loading eggs onto Cole's plate.

"Sheriff called this morning. Said he figured you boys might not volunteer the information." Pa gave Seth one of his special looks—the one that said, *you can't keep anything from me.*

"We didn't want to worry you for no reason," I volunteered, as I poured a cup of coffee. "It was nothing. Harmony was frightened and called the sheriff before Seth and I knew she'd done it."

When Seth finally glanced my way, his expression changed. "Damn, Liam. You don't look so good."

Pa lowered his newspaper and studied me for the first time. His hair was well beyond grey now. Black-rimmed reading glasses sat low on his nose and his face always had redness to it. Leathery creases etched his friendly face from years of working in the sun. The eyes that watched me with concern, were faded blue and glossy.

Even though he was already advanced in age when he and Molly adopted us, he'd aged the most over the past year. Her death was hard on all of us, but I believe she took a piece of his heart and soul with her.

"You don't look well, Liam. Are you sick, son?" Pa asked, laying his paper on the table before coming to stand in front of me. Pa wasn't a tall man in stature, but what he lacked in physical mass, he surpassed in character. Paul McKenzie was a man of his word, and someone my brothers and I aspire to be like.

"Maybe just a little. I'll be fine. Think I'll pass on breakfast though." Pa raised his hand to my forehead. His eyebrows knitted together in concern. I must have been as hot as I felt.

"You'll not be working today, Liam. If you're not eating breakfast, get yourself back up to bed. I'll check on you after I feed the hogs," Pa said, turning back to his seat. Seth had placed a plate of eggs, bacon, and toast on the table for him.

"I'll be okay. I just need to get moving, that's all," I tried to assure him.

"No. You'll do as I say. Off to bed. And I don't care if you're nineteen. Nineteen doesn't automatically give you common sense and a road map." He left no room for argument, and I didn't have enough energy to argue, anyway. Couldn't remember ever feeling this sick. I carried my cup full of coffee back up to my bedroom.

"Don't worry about your chores, Liam. Seth and I will do them," Cole yelled from the kitchen.

"Speak for yourself," I heard Seth grumble. "It was his day to make breakfast."

Ignoring it all, I closed the bedroom door, pulled the blinds to darken the room, and collapsed onto the bed. I didn't want to sleep. The nightmare was stirring at the edges of my fevered mind and the last thing I wanted was to go anywhere near that dream again.

THREE

I DON'T KNOW how long I slept. With the blinds closed, it made it difficult to tell the time. Thankfully, there were no more dreams. I picked up my cell phone. It was after three in the afternoon.

How could I have slept the day away like that?

At least I felt better. Not one hundred percent, but better. I had just sat up in bed when someone knocked softly on the door before easing it open.

Harmony walked into my room wearing a printed skirt, denim jacket, and western boots. She carried a tray with one hand, balancing it on her hip as she managed the door.

"I heard you were sick. Since you didn't answer my messages, I figured it was bad." Her smile could light up the darkest room. Seeing her face was all the medicine I needed.

I patted the bed beside me. "Hey, beautiful. What did you bring me?"

She set the tray with a steaming bowl of soup on my lap, then sat on the edge of the bed. "Mom made a big pot of chicken noodle soup when I told her you were sick." Harmony tucked her long brown hair behind one of her ears and watched me.

"Your mom is almost as sweet as you. This is great. I'm feeling a little better, but I haven't eaten all day. Thank you." I ate several spoonfuls of soup and contentment spread through me with each delicious mouthful. I hadn't realized how hungry I was.

Harmony unwrapped a large bun that resembled a loaf of French bread and tore off a piece for me. In no time, I had polished off the bowl of soup and bread. Harmony simply watched me with a pleased look on her face.

When I finished, she took the tray and set it on my dresser, then returned to sit next to me on the bed. She picked up my bible that was on my nightstand and thumbed through it briefly before returning it to where she found it.

I hadn't been good about reading it since Ma died, which was apparent from the thin layer of dust on the cover.

"Feel like getting some fresh air?" she asked.

I did. My strength was returning, so lying in bed didn't feel right anymore. She handed me my jeans with a smile before taking the tray and leaving the room. I pulled my jeans on and grabbed a clean t-shirt, pulling it over my head as I made my way down the stairs.

The old house was quiet. My brothers and father were all working around the farm. A twinge of guilt plagued me as I thought of my brothers doing my work on top of their own.

I found Harmony sitting on the front porch

swing, rocking slightly and staring off into the distance. In my opinion, she was the prettiest girl in town. I'd known her since we were kids, back when I used to pull her hair and make her cry—something she never let me forget. When I first noticed her differently, she was a freshman, but not as silly as most girls her age. But it was her unwavering confidence that drew me to her.

I joined her on the swing and we started a gentle rhythm. We stared at the scenery together, like we had so many times before. Her hand in mine felt right.

Even behind her warm smile, I knew there was something on her mind. I had a good idea of what it might be.

"Last night, before I took the trash out, you said you wanted to talk about something with me," I said.

She squeezed my hand before letting it go to stand and walk a few feet away. "I was offered another scholarship." She wasn't looking at me when she spoke.

That same ache in my gut returned. We'd had this discussion before. She wanted to go away to college and she wanted me to go with her. It sounded good, and in my heart, I wanted to.

"Where?" I asked.

"California. Berkeley." She leaned against the wood post of the porch and crossed her arms over her chest. "Come with me. I know you can qualify for several scholarships, and I'll help you apply for grants as well. If you get a part-time job, I know we can make it work."

I could barely look at her hopeful expression. It hurt my heart. "Harmony, we've been over this before. You know why I can't leave."

Her expression turned to one of frustration. "Why? Because your pa can't run the farm without you? Because if you go, Seth may not take advantage of his athletic scholarship? Because the burden of the work would fall on Cole, and he's too young for that sort of responsibility? How many other excuses have you found, Liam?" Her words were harsh, but her eyes were glossy as if she'd cry at any moment. I hated to see her cry. Worse than that, I hated to be the reason.

"Harmony—" I said before she cut me off.

"Enough, Liam. Enough with your excuses. Your pa is a wonderful man and your ma was the best of 'em. He should retire, sell off the farm so you boys can move on. Have you taken a good look at him lately? He's moving slower and slower. Most men his age have given up hard labor. Isn't it time that you talked to him about retiring? Why is he still holding on?" she asked, but I had the feeling she was merely fleshing out her own thoughts out loud.

"He planned to retire with Ma, but after she passed, he never talked about it again. It's like he needed the farm to keep going. I'm afraid if we force him to sell off the land and stop farming for a living, he'll go downhill fast." The very thought had my eyes stinging, so I got up to pace around the porch.

"You know what they did for us boys. I can't simply walk away from that. If I did, I know Seth wouldn't take that scholarship. He'd stay. And if we both left, Cole would no doubt carry the brunt of it all, during a time that should be fun and carefree. I won't sacrifice their happiness for my own. I'm not built that way."

I could see the pain my decision was causing her. Damned if I do, and damned if I don't.

She wiped at her eyes. "You sacrifice for everyone, Liam—everyone but me." Her eyes were shiny, but I recognized the set of her jaw. And I knew she'd made a choice.

"I've waited a year for you because I didn't want to leave you when Molly passed. But I'm not certain what I'm waiting for anymore. You have your priorities, Liam. It's time for me to reconsider mine." She walked over to me and reached up on her tip-toes to kiss my lips. Her thumb wiped away the single tear that had slid down my cheek. She hugged me tightly then.

"I will always love you, Liam. We never forget our first love. And I was so certain you'd be my last."

When she pulled out of my arms, her eyes were brimming with tears. She quickly turned and ran down the porch steps and got into her hard-topped Jeep and drove away.

I watched her leave down the long dirt road until I couldn't see her anymore. My mind was having its own war. A huge part of me wanted to turn my back on this life and chase after her. It was no secret that I wanted to marry her as soon as we both finished school.

But I held off a year to help Pa get things ready for retirement and then Ma left us and there I was.

Harmony was right, Pa was looking like he'd aged ten more years, and for a seventy-year-old man, that wasn't a good thing. I'd noticed, but I hadn't had the time to put two and two together. Maybe I did need to push the issue with him for his own good.

If I could convince him it's time, maybe I'd still have a chance with Harmony.

From one of the western fields, I could see Pa's truck kicking up dust as he made his way to the house. He was driving much faster than normal. Ordinarily, he drove like a turtle to save the suspension and shocks from wear and tear. Farm life was hard on vehicles.

Yes, he was driving way too fast. Something was wrong. I walked down the steps to meet him as the truck pulled up in front of the house. Pa's face was redder than normal, and he had a thin layer of perspiration on his brow, even though the air wasn't too hot.

I walked quickly up to the truck and Pa rolled the window down. "You feeling better?" he asked. I nodded. "Good. Hop in. Your brothers at the hospital."

I ran around the truck and jumped into the passenger seat. "Which brother?" I asked.

"Seth. Someone beat him up pretty bad, from what I hear. They didn't give me many details, but I want to get there quickly." Pa put the truck in gear and sped down the same road I'd watched Harmony leave by a few minutes earlier.

Seth was no push-over. I was having a difficult time imagining anyone getting the upper hand on him. Especially, to land him in the hospital.

"I thought Seth was here. Where was he when it happened?"

Pa glanced at me briefly. "I sent him to town for some groceries. I was trying to give him a break. He was working hard all day." Pa shook his head.

I wasn't certain what they told Pa, but he drove in silence, breaking the speed limit the entire way.

CHAPTER
FOUR

WHEN WE REACHED THE HOSPITAL, the sheriff was waiting for us. He shook our hands briefly. "Sorry to be meeting over something like this, Paul. I've been meaning to stop in at your place for a cup of coffee. Summer has all the kids getting into trouble, and now this. I don't need outsiders making more problems," he said as he led us into the Lake Cumberland Regional Hospital.

"How's my boy?" Pa asked, ignoring the small talk.

"He'll be all right. The docs were worried he'd punctured a lung and possibly other internal injuries when they brought him in, but it appears to be no more than a cracked rib and a lot of scrapes and bruises. I think he got lucky," the sheriff said as he pushed open the door to Seth's room.

The sheriff made Seth's injuries sound minor, so I was hardly prepared for how bad he looked. I stopped just past the door, while Pa and the sheriff continued to Seth's bed.

He was propped up on a couple of pillows. A

third was tucked under his left arm and wedged against his body. Seth's face was swollen with black and blue bruises around both eyes and along his right cheek and jaw.

My stomach felt sick again and my head began to pound. My reaction was so strong that I rushed into the toilet closet and threw up. Pa came to the door and asked if I was okay.

"I'm fine. Must still be sick."

He patted me on the back and left the bathroom. I splashed water on my face and rinsed my mouth before going back into the room. When I returned, the sheriff looked amused.

"Delicate stomach, Liam?" he teased.

Pa glanced at me. "No, he's been sick." He turned his attention back to Seth.

Pa was gripping Seth's hand in his. I thought Seth was sleeping, but then one of his eyes opened a fraction to look at me. I felt awful for him, and somehow responsible. Maybe because I wasn't there to protect him.

"Don't look so worried, big brother. You should see the other guys." Seth tried to laugh at his own joke but ended up wincing in pain instead.

I moved past the sheriff to stand on the opposite side of the bed from Pa. I tried to smile and put a hand on his shoulder but quickly pulled it back when even that light touch made him wince in pain. That's when I pulled the sheet back.

"Good lord!" muttered the sheriff. He turned and left the room, speaking into the radio attached to his shoulder. I guess it took seeing the extent of

Seth's injuries for him to take the attack more seriously.

Seth's body was cut, scraped, and bruised badly enough to have been in a serious hit and run. Somebody did this to him. They could have killed him. My shock was beginning to turn to something else. *Rage.*

I looked at Pa and saw that his eyes were shiny with tears. He was fighting hard not to let go. "What happened, son?"

Seth closed his eyes. "It was the guys from the diner. I was walking out of the grocery with my arms full. They confronted me in the parking lot and wouldn't let me get to the car. They kept talking about crazy stuff like, the name of my pack, how many were in it, and who had been hiding us...crazy shit." Pa's expression changed, and he looked as though he was deep in thought.

"How many were there?" I asked, trying to control the shaking in my hands and the tremor in my voice.

"More than five. Six or seven, maybe."

"This was the same bunch who were causing trouble at the diner?" Pa asked, looking more in control of his emotions.

"The same—with friends." Seth turned his head on the pillow and closed his eyes.

As if on cue, a cute nurse wearing blue scrubs printed with smiley faces entered the room. "This one needs some rest. One of you may stay if you wish, but I can assure you, his injuries are superficial and not life-threatening. He just doesn't look real pretty right now."

"Nobody needs to stay with me. I just had the ass-kicking of a lifetime. Probably karma catching up to me. I'll live," Seth added. "Is it time for my sponge bath?" He gave the nurse a lopsided smile that was meant to be charming but looked disturbing instead.

The nurse rolled her eyes and laughed. "You're not getting a sponge bath, *Romeo*. You'll be released in the morning." She was still looking over his chart when we nodded at Seth, then turned to leave.

"Liam," Seth called.

Pa had already walked out ahead of me, so I paused and turned back.

"They mentioned Cole—by name." Seth's point was clear as glass.

I nodded my understanding. We had always looked after Cole, with him being the youngest, and frankly, the most trusting of us all. He'd just finished his sophomore year of high school and had his heart broken twice already. It was my responsibility to protect my brothers.

I caught up with Pa down the hall and we walked silently through the maze of seemingly endless corridors until we reached the entrance. The sun was lower in the sky and the approaching evening felt ominous for some reason. Maybe it was seeing my brother in the hospital like that. Maybe something else.

As we exited the building, I saw the sheriff speaking with two deputies. When he noticed us, he left them and came over to follow us to Pa's truck.

"Paul, I've got every available man looking for these guys. We'll catch them. Don't you worry."

Pa stopped just before getting into the truck. Cole pulled up in Seth's Civic and jumped out quickly. "What's happened? Where's Seth?" His worried expression looked near panic.

I was relieved to see him unharmed. "He's fine…well, not fine, but he'll be all right. They're keeping him overnight," I said.

The sheriff's face scrunched up like he was thinking hard. "Do you have your license, Cole?"

Cole looked guiltily at Pa and then the sheriff. "No, sir. I have my permit, and since I drive with Seth a lot, I have his spare keys. When I got Liam's message, I was in the cornfield working on a broken water line. I asked a neighbor to give me a ride into town. I found Seth's car at the grocery and drove it over. It was only a few miles." He shuffled nervously from one foot to the other.

The sheriff shook his head.

"Liam, you drive Cole home. I'm going to speak to the sheriff a bit," Pa said.

I wanted to be in on this conversation, but I knew better than to argue with him, especially in front of others. I nodded and took the keys from Cole.

"Can't I see him?" Cole asked.

"He'll be fine. You can see him in the morning when we pick him up. I want you to stay with me. Let's get some take-out for dinner. Your choice."

Cole looked disappointed but got in the passenger side anyway. "See you at home, Pa," I said.

Pa nodded at me and Cole and I drove out of

the parking lot of the hospital and headed into town to find some food.

Pa wasn't the type to leave us out of anything. It was unusual for him to send us home now. I'd planned to press him on the matter when he returned.

I filled Cole in on everything that I knew about what had happened, which wasn't much. It appeared that this gang had singled us out for some reason but for the life of me, I didn't know why. We hadn't done anything to provoke them, at least that I could think of.

Cole and I grabbed some fried chicken, mashed potatoes with gravy, and coleslaw for dinner. We had leftover green beans to warm up at home. Cole and I ate quietly, both lost in our own private thoughts about the recent events.

"You still having those nightmares?" Cole asked, avoiding eye contact.

I'd been having nightmares on and off for the last month or so. Every time, I'd wake drenched in sweat, my heart racing, and an awful feeling of dread that took a while to shake off. The dreams were sporadic with no obvious reason or cause.

"Had one last night. Worst one yet." I smiled at him and ruffled his hair to lighten the mood. "They're just dreams. Nothing to worry about. Harmony thinks I'm allergic to dairy." Remembering her cure to my nightmares made me chuckle. Cole also thought the idea was funny.

"Her sister said she's leaving for California. Is that true?" Cole looked uncomfortable asking.

"When did she tell you that?"

"Yesterday. Is it true? Is Harmony leaving?" Cole pressed.

So, she had already made up her mind. I can't say I blamed her. Deep down, I knew she'd only stayed behind for me. I didn't want to hold her back, but I didn't want her to go, either.

"I guess so." I occupied myself with cleaning up the table. We had left a plate in the oven for Pa, but he hadn't returned yet.

"What are you going to do? Aren't you in love with her?" Cole's question surprised me.

"I don't know. And yeah, I've been in love with Harmony for a while."

Cole looked thoughtful for a moment. "You should go with her."

"It's not that easy, Cole."

"It should be." I looked up from piling the dishes into the sink. Cole had a serious look on his face that made him suddenly seem older than his almost sixteen years.

"But it's not. I haven't decided what I'll do yet. I'd planned to talk to Pa about selling off some of the lands so he can retire from farming. What do you think about that?" I asked.

Cole followed me into the living room where I plopped down into Ma's chair. We still called it that—Ma's chair. I could still smell her every time I sat in it. Rose water was her favorite scent.

Cole walked over to the stereo and turned on some soft classical music. We all missed her and had our own small ways to keep her with us. Ma always had classical music playing. Sometimes she'd let us play country music, but not for long.

"I thought that was the plan all along." Cole laid himself across the couch, put his hands behind his head, and crossed his legs at the ankle.

"It was, but since Ma left, he hasn't mentioned it, and hasn't done anything about it. I figured he needed the work to take his mind off her." We were silent for a long time.

"Whatever you do, don't stay for me. I'd miss you, but I'll be just fine," Cole said.

"Who said you have anything to do with it?" I teased.

"Please. Everyone in town knows who my big brothers are. I know you and Seth try to keep me out of trouble. It's not a secret." Cole grinned at me. "But seriously, don't put your life on hold for me. I don't want that on my shoulders."

I looked at him thoughtfully. He really was more aware of what was happening around him than anyone gave him credit for. I turned on the TV and began flipping through the channels to find something to watch.

It was just past nine o'clock and Pa still wasn't home. Maybe he decided to stay with Seth, after all.

CHAPTER
FIVE

EARLY MORNING SUNLIGHT filled the living room. My face was buried into the couch where I must have fallen asleep. Thankfully, I had no dreams. If I dreamed or didn't dream had become the gauge by how I evaluated a good night's sleep. With no dreams to haunt me, I dragged myself from the couch to follow the smell of breakfast cooking in the kitchen.

Pa was standing at the stove, moving eggs around in a skillet. Bacon, toast and a bowl of fruit were already on the table. Since we all rose early each day, the kitchen was usually a busy place. Not this morning.

"Good morning," I said while pouring a cup of coffee.

Pa glanced over his shoulder. "Good morning, Liam. Did you sleep well?"

I took the juice from the fridge and set it on the table. "Not bad, considering I slept on the couch. What time did you come home?"

He didn't answer right away. Pa carried the

skillet of eggs to the table and used the spatula to serve some for the two of us. I waited for him to join me.

"Late. I stopped off to see a friend and then went to Charlie's for a drink." Pa sat down and began buttering his toast. He rarely drank, and it was unusual for him to go to the bar without friends or something to celebrate.

"I've already called about Seth. They said he's doing better than they expected. The doctor already made his rounds and said he could go home anytime. I'll pick him up after breakfast," Pa said.

"I can get him."

"No. It seems like this gang has it out for you and your brothers. I'd like for the three of you to lay low for a while. Let the sheriff find these guys or confirm they've moved on. They're not locals, so it's possible they've left town already. The sheriff can't figure out where they're staying, but he's had multiple sightings. Every time the authorities show up, they disappear. They can't stay under the radar forever," Pa said.

I didn't like the sound of that. These guys caused all sorts of trouble, but we're the ones under house arrest. "But Pa, tomorrow's the Fourth of July celebration. Seth, Cole, and I were planning to go. I'm taking Harmony too," I said. I wasn't one hundred percent certain Harmony still wanted to go with me anymore.

"I don't think it's a good idea," Pa said as he stared at his food.

Cole came into the kitchen with tons of energy, as usual. I always thought I was a morning person, but Cole could make me question that assumption. He was usually bouncing off the walls even before he had coffee. "Morning, family!" Cole exclaimed, ruffling my hair and slapping Pa on the back.

"Morning," I grumbled.

"Good morning, Cole. I guess we don't need to ask how you slept," Pa said, chuckling.

Cole sat down with a plate full of food that made ours look like we're on a diet. That kid could put away the food. Ma used to say that I did the same thing at his age, but I don't remember.

"Pa wants us to lay low until they catch that gang or they move on." I watched for Cole's reaction.

"What? Tomorrow's Independence Day. I've been waiting for months for this." Cole's entire demeanor seemed to deflate.

"Maybe if you promise to stay together—" Pa began.

"We do!" Cole jumped out of his seat and did his version of a victory dance. I felt like joining him, but I had no plans to hang out with my brothers the entire day and night. I wanted some time alone with Harmony if she'd have me.

"All right. But then I want your butts glued to our land until this blows over. I guess there'll be enough people around to keep you three out of trouble," Pa said, then took a sip of his coffee.

"Deal," Cole said, before sitting down and inhaling his food faster than it took me to finish my eggs. Watching Cole eat was like watching a sporting event. It was hard to look away.

Cole was done and out the door before my first

cup of coffee was finished. Once again, it was just Pa and me. He wasn't reading his paper as he usually did after he finished eating breakfast. He kept staring at the steam coming from his second cup of coffee.

That got me thinking. "Pa. Who did you go see last night, and what did you and the sheriff talk about?"

He looked up from his preoccupation with his cup to stare at me a moment. "I went to see the lawyer who arranged your adoptions for us."

This was not what I expected to hear. "Why?"

Pa toyed with his cup. "Something you and Seth said about these guys. It's most likely nothing, but I didn't want to be caught off guard if there was something in your past that might come back to hurt you."

"I thought we were abandoned and nobody knew who our real parents were," I said, a knot forming in my throat. Something had Pa shook up and he was a hard man to rattle.

"That's true, mostly. Nobody knew the name of your parents or where you came from. You didn't turn up in any missing person database, which was strange, considering there were three of you." Pa seemed to be lost in a memory and I tried hard to wait patiently for his reply, but a sense of urgency was making me anxious.

"What do you mean by 'mostly'? What aren't you telling me, Pa?"

"Your ma—Molly—didn't want you to know about your real ma until you were older. She felt it might harm you all to know such a tragic thing too early." He looked sad and it tugged at my heart, but I needed to know anything he knew about our past.

"Pa."

He took a deep breath and let it out. His wrinkles seemed deeper and his hair was almost white now. A year ago, it was salt and peppered, but now it was as white as it could be.

"We told you that you three were left at an orphanage, but that's not true. It was a little white lie created to erase the ugly truth." Pa took another sip of coffee and pushed his plate away.

"It was big news in Tennessee. Three children found in a remote area of woods. It wasn't even that they found you boys alone. Children are abandoned every day, unfortunately." Pa was looking more and more uncomfortable telling his story and I was more and more entranced by his every word.

"What made it so sensational was that you were found in the woods, next to a woman who died violently. Her body had been bitten and torn. They said she must have been attacked by a wild animal, but the autopsy was inconclusive." He watched my face as his words sunk in.

We had a mother. And she died, most likely in our presence. That same sickness I'd been battling came back with a vengeance. I jumped up, knocking the chair over before running to the sink to throw up. When I was done, I felt Pa's hand on my shoulder. He handed me a clean cloth to wipe my mouth.

"I'm sorry, Liam. I dreaded telling you this story for years. It's a horrible thing to hear. I always thought Molly would be here when I did." Pa hugged me quickly and walked out of the room. I heard the front door open and close.

A few minutes later, I found him on the front porch packing his pipe with tobacco. The morning air was still cool. The wood slats of the porch creaked and groaned as I stepped. I sat on the porch swing, wondering if it was better not knowing. Now I'd be cursed with questions—why were we there? Did she die protecting us? Did she suffer? What was she like? Who was she?

"Why wasn't anyone looking for a woman and her three children?" The notion was unfathomable in this day and age of information. Surely, someone knew us. And they must have seen the news if it was as publicized as Pa said. I had no reason to doubt him. Pa wasn't the sort of man to embellish anything for the sake of the story.

He finished lighting his pipe and blew smoke that drifted on the air around his head. He reached into the front pocket of his flannel shirt and pulled out a picture that he handed to me. "This is all they knew. She was in her late twenties-early thirties, long brown hair, and had that tattoo on the back of her shoulder."

I studied the photo. It was an abstract symbol of a wolf's head that wrapped around itself like the smoke from Pa's pipe. On closer inspection, I realized the smoke was really flames forming the shape that may have represented the moon.

My heartfelt tight knowing that this was a picture from *her* shoulder. It was like almost being able to touch her but knowing I never would. "Did they show this tattoo in the news?" I asked, still holding the photo.

"Yes, but not a word. They were hoping someone would recognize the art, to give them a lead, but nothing came of it. It was all very sad and peculiar at the same time." Pa held the pipe in his lips and stared out across the fields that made up our farm.

"If this happened in Tennessee, how did you and ma end up adopting us?"

"That was all your mother's doing. Most of the story she told you was true. She didn't visit an orphanage, but she fell in love with three little boys when she heard the news. She pulled strings I didn't even know she had. Molly even reached out to an old boyfriend from college to make it happen." He smiled as he spoke about Ma.

It was the only good thing about this conversation—watching Pa remember the woman we all loved and missed.

"The next thing I knew, we had three boys to raise, and I had no idea what to do with you. But she did. And she helped me figure it out along the way. She loved you boys at first sight, but it didn't take me long to feel the same." His eyes became glossy again.

"You boys filled a place in my heart that I didn't know was empty." He wiped his eyes with the back of his sleeve. I went to him and wrapped my arms around him and he let me.

"I love you, Pa. We all do. My wanting to know about our past doesn't change the fact that you're our father and Molly was our mother."

He squeezed me tight before releasing me. "Thank you, Liam," Pa said, then laid his pipe on the little table on the porch. "I'm going to get your brother. You can decide how and when to tell them."

Pa climbed down the stairs more carefully than I'd ever seen him do. He walked to his truck and climbed in. I headed to the barn to start my share of the chores with a heavy heart. It was up to me to share this news of our birth mother and our haunted past with my brothers. I could see why Pa dreaded the conversation. Telling the truth doesn't always set you free.

What really had me shaken was my mother's tattoo. I'd seen it several times in my dreams but didn't understand it. I may have even seen my mother. Now the dreams I'd been dreading could be a window into my past. Maybe they've actually suppressed memories. I had no memories before coming here. That was all I've ever known. Could I have locked them away?

And, do I really want to know what's hidden in the memories of a troubled childhood?

CHAPTER
SIX

THE FOURTH of July was a huge celebration in Summerset. It felt like the entire town turned out for the festivities. It always started with a parade down Main Street that circled what was considered the town center.

People would come early to leave folding chairs, umbrellas, and even canopies to stake out their spot to watch the parade from. We were no exception. There were only a few spots on the parade route that had alleys, and we always snagged one of them as our spot.

Even before doing our chores, Cole drove Seth's car and followed me in my truck. The streets were mostly deserted with the exception of the handful of people setting up their items, meant to hold their tiny bit of real estate for the first of the day's events.

The streets were decorated with U.S. flags on every light pole and building. While other people used chairs and coolers to hold their spot, we used my truck. I turned into the alley and parked the

truck with the tailgate facing the street. We drove
back with Seth's car to get the work done before
the parade and barbecue began. It was a great in-
centive to breeze through our chores.

I considered telling my brothers of the grim secret I'd learned the day before but decided it could
wait another day. No sense ruining one of the best
days of the year with bad news. There was no new
information about the motorcycle gang, and for the
life of me, I couldn't understand how a group that
large, on loud bikes, could continue to slip under
the radar.

It was only a matter of time before their luck
ran out and they'd be arrested for assaulting Seth
and threatening Harmony and me. There was
little concern that they'd show up today. Too
many witnesses—the entire sheriff's department
was milling about to ensure a peaceful celebration.

Breakfast was ready when we returned and
there was an excited buzz around the table. "I can't
wait to buy one of Mrs. Brown's chocolate cream
pies," Cole said as he grabbed the last two pieces
of bacon.

Mrs. Brown won the baking contest every year,
and for good reason. Her baked goods were well
known around this part of the state. She'd even
won the blue ribbon in the Kentucky State Fair
once. It was the sort of food you'd have dreams
about. It was that good.

"Better get to her booth early. They go fast." Pa
took out a twenty-dollar bill from his money-clip
and handed it to Cole. "Get one of her cherry pies,

as well. Your ma loved cherry pie." Cole took the bill and smiled at Pa.

Seth was smiling at the conversation but was uncharacteristically quiet this morning. When he returned from the hospital, he went to his room to rest and didn't come out until the evening meal.

"You're healing nicely, Seth," I said, passing him the last piece of toast.

He shook his head. "Yeah, the doc said I was the fastest healer he'd ever seen." His words didn't match his demeanor.

"You okay?" I asked.

"Yeah, I'll be fine. My head has been hurting and I've been feeling sick to my stomach since they beat the crap out of me." He looked at me then. "And I've had some bad dreams the last two nights. Maybe that whoop'n shook me up a little." Seth almost looked embarrassed to admit it.

"Don't worry about it. That was a serious ass kicking. They could have killed you. Nothing to take lightly," I said, reaching over to clasp his shoulder. He didn't flinch this time.

"What did you dream?" Cole asked, totally oblivious to Seth's discomfort about the topic.

Seth hesitated. "It was weird shit."

"Seth," Pa warned.

"Sorry, Pa." Seth looked at me. "It was all jumbled up and most of it didn't make a lick of sense, but I remember one thing I can't get out of my head."

For some unknown reason, I was nervous to hear that Seth was having bad dreams. "What?" I pressed.

"An enormous wolf with green eyes." Seth was staring at his coffee like he was back in the dream.

"That don't sound scary," Cole said as he began to gather the dishes.

"I have to agree with Cole," Pa said, joining the conversation from behind his newspaper.

"I didn't say it was scary. It was sad. The wolf was sad, broken-hearted, even."

Pa lowered his paper and watched Seth, who was still staring at his empty coffee cup. "Why was the wolf sad, Seth?"

"She had to leave her cubs."

I stared at Seth. His dream sounded warning bells in my head. But why?

Cole walked over from the sink, wiping his hands on a towel. "How do you know that she was sad or that she had to leave her cubs?"

Seth looked at each of us in turn. "It was like she spoke to me, but without any words." He shook his head. "I can't explain it. But it really got to me for some reason."

When he realized how intently we were staring at him, he cracked a typical Seth smile and got up from the table slowly. "It's probably from those pain meds the doc has me on. I should stop taking them. Pretty sure I could do most of my chores today."

"Not so fast. You'll take it easy another day, and then we'll see what the doctor says. Liam and Cole will do your chores until we get the green light from your doctor." Pa drank the last sip of his coffee and stood up.

"Better get at it, boys," Pa said as he left the

kitchen. "And don't forget the rule about staying together at the celebration."

Cole rolled his eyes and Seth shook his head. Hanging out together was fine for a few hours, but then we all had different friends and interests that would pull us in different directions. I certainly didn't want these two clowns hanging around Harmony and me the entire day. We'd have to find a compromise that didn't totally break Pa's rule about staying together—maybe stretch it a bit.

When the cows and horses were fed, the last water line was repaired, and the resting field was somewhat plowed, Seth and I showered and dressed in clean jeans, t-shirts, and boots. Cole wore sneakers and cut-off denim shorts. Pa said he'd make an appearance at the barbecue, but then he'd come back home. He wasn't much for big parties anymore.

The three of us piled into Seth's car and headed into town. It was a fast thirty-minute drive. Most of the roads were narrow and winding through thick canopies of trees that hung over the road, only allowing bits of sunlight to stream in like laser beams as we drove.

Closer to town the trees fell away, offering a more open view of scattered farms, fields, barns, and houses. Even closer in, the farms disappeared, and the housing became denser.

We had a cooler with beer and soda—beer hidden under the ice and sodas on top in case anyone looked. Pa never condoned getting drunk, but he had no problem with us having a beer or two. Maybe that was why we rarely overindulged. If we abused the privilege, Pa would have taken away the option, along with any free time that allowed us to get into trouble in the first place.

We picked up Harmony and her friend Lisa. It was tight in the Civic with three good-sized guys and the two girls, but it was a short drive from Harmony's house to the downtown area.

"What the hell happened to you?" Lisa asked Seth, once we started driving.

Harmony must not have told her. "He got jumped by the same motorcycle gang that threatened Harmony and me the other night." I attempted to relax the tension in my neck from the mere mention of what had occurred.

"That's terrible. I hope they catch those losers," Lisa said, frowning.

"I don't think they have, but hopefully they've left town. That's what the sheriff said," Harmony replied.

Seth didn't say a word. He hadn't been himself since it happened. Can't say I blamed him. I wasn't over it, myself. Protecting those I loved had become a preoccupation with me in the last few days.

After parking a few blocks away in the Walmart parking lot, we walked to where we had left my truck. The streets were filled with people.

We had to evict some middle school kids who had taken up residence in the back of the truck.

They pouted and threw a few insults over their shoulders as they went. Cole acted like he was going to chase them, and they ran away. The look of fear on their faces gave us a good laugh.

There was country music over the loud-speakers and people dancing in the roped-off sections of the streets while we all waited for the parade to pass by. Seth and the girls sat on the tailgate with their legs swinging back and forth. Cole and I stood, talking to different people we knew as they passed by. We kept our beers and sodas in snuggies so people had no idea what we were drinking.

Kids with their faces painted and waving flags or water pistols were everywhere. I was squirted at least ten times in a one-hour period. By that time the sun was directly overhead, and it was starting to get hot, so I didn't mind the water. Cole got smart and started encouraging kids to shoot him with water.

The mood was festive, everyone was smiling, and the parade wasn't half-bad this year. At least none of them fell over. Even Harmony seemed happy. I was worried that she would leave me, cold-turkey. I let her know when I asked if she still wanted to go with me, that I wanted to talk about everything that was going on.

The day of the celebration, she looked like a country boy's dream. She had a snug-fitting red and white checked blouse that dipped low on her chest, but just enough to stay classy. Her cut-off denim skirt was short and showed off her long muscular legs from years of running track in high school.

When we picked her up, she was wearing cowboy boots, but she'd already switched them out for a pair of flip-flops. I knew she'd put the boots back on for dancing that night.

After the parade passed, Cole took Lisa to get an iced tea, because the beer and soda we had wasn't good enough. Seth was talking to a group of seniors from his graduating class, so I sat next to Harmony and held her hand. She leaned her head on my shoulder. "I'm going to miss this," she said.

"About that." She raised her head to look at me. "I don't want to lose you, Harmony."

"And I don't want to lose you. So, what are we going to do about it?" She smiled at me with those full cherry lips of hers.

I kissed her, long and deep. She responded to the kiss by wrapping her arms around my neck and pulling me closer. It had always felt this right, this perfect with Harmony. I believed there could never be another person in the world who could make me feel this way. *How could I let that go?*

She broke our kiss but held my face in her hands. "I'm leaving for California in a few days. I want you to go with me." She pleaded with her eyes.

"I want to be with you, but I can't leave that soon. I still need to talk to Pa, help him make arrangements, and run the farm until it sells. That's assuming he'll go along with it."

"Then do it. Start the conversation with him.

You can come to California as soon as it's settled." She stroked my cheek. "But I won't wait forever, Liam."

"I know. I'll speak to him tomorrow." I released her and watched the crowds dispersing.

"Promise?"

"Promise."

Volunteers were taking down the yellow barrier tape and others were scooping up animal crap from the streets. The barbecue had already started, but there was always more than enough food.

Cole and Lisa walked up, with her holding a large generic paper cup. We looked at her. "It's sweet tea! So good. Want some?" She held out the cup and we shook our heads.

Seth made his way back to the truck. "Let's go before all the food is gone."

Nobody was worried about that, but Harmony and Lisa got into the cab of the truck with me, while Cole and Seth climbed into the back and sat on the sides of the truck's bed, holding on to the roof of the cab.

We drove to Summersport Park where the cookout was held. After purchasing our tickets, we meandered, as a group, to various booths to sample everything our tickets would allow. Since the girls didn't use all their food tickets, Seth and Cole went back for seconds.

Somehow, we ended up in a water balloon fight where everyone, but Lisa were soaked. When her ex showed up, we didn't see her for the rest of the day. Cole and Seth were playing on teams in a bean-bag-toss competition across the field and

Harmony and I laid on a blanket she had brought in an effort to dry off in the sun.

Mostly we just kissed and messed around. Life was good and for the first time in the last year, I felt lighter and freer than I had in awhile. Yes, I would talk to Pa. I'd get him back on track with selling and retiring, Seth would go to college to play football and get his education. Cole wouldn't have the weight of the farm on him while he finished high school and decided what he wanted to do with his life. I would start a new beginning with Harmony.

I'd always wanted to be a firefighter, but Pa advised me to get a degree first, then pursue that career, if I still wanted to. I agreed. If worse came to worst, I could try to get on with one of the fire departments in California to help pay for Harmony's education while I took classes part-time.

It could all work out.

CHAPTER
SEVEN

THE NIGHT SKY was lit up with a rainbow of colors when the fireworks show began. Harmony sat between my outstretched legs, with her back resting against my chest as we enjoyed the long-standing American tradition, the hallmark of most independence celebrations.

Proud to Be an American could be heard over the loud-speakers and occasionally the voice of the late president, Ronald Reagan, giving one of his speeches about freedom. It filled me with pride and made me consider once again the notion of serving a term in the military. I'd always wanted to and believed I would but wasn't certain where it would fit with college and career.

"This is my favorite time of year," Harmony announced.

I squeezed her tighter. "I know."

"Mine too," Cole said, with a mouth full of fried chicken.

Seth, who had his arm around a pretty blonde

girl he introduced as Leigh, laughed at Cole. "You'll be in a food-coma tomorrow."

It was amazing that as bruised as Seth was, he could still find willing girls to cuddle with. At least he was smiling. He'd been a bit distant, which wasn't Seth at all.

Seth was a big-time player. He never settled for one girl, but he never lied to them. He just wouldn't commit. And again, and again, girls would try to change that well-known fact. He was a good-looking guy, football star, with much darker coloring than Cole or me. With contrasting blue eyes, the ladies were always chasing him. And Seth liked it that way.

The fireworks lasted twenty or thirty minutes. Cheers and whistles from the crowd finally died down and everyone started talking to one another or packing up their chairs, coolers, and blankets. Many were trying to gather up their kids, who were running all over the park, having a grand old time. I could remember doing the same with my brothers.

We carried our stuff back to my truck and drove to the high school, where they were hosting the annual Fourth of July Dance for anyone who purchased advance tickets, which we had done months earlier. The tickets for the dance sold out early every year. It was the biggest community event, next to the Christmas celebration, that Summerset had.

We'd barely walked in the door when Cole and Seth ditched us to find their friends. Alone with Harmony, I took her hand and led her onto the dance floor that was already packed with people. Some pop song with a good beat was playing and we danced through three more songs before the DJ played a slow one.

I held her in my arms and she reached up to pull my head down to hers. Our lips met and everything else melted away. All the distractions were pushed from my mind with a single kiss. My body was suddenly alive with pent-up energy, and Harmony felt so good in my arms. I pulled her tightly against me.

When she pulled away, I realized we'd stopped dancing. I smiled sheepishly. She took my hand and led me off the dance floor to a dark place at the back of the bleachers. Memories from high school came to mind as I let her guide me. She looked back and smiled at me over her shoulder and my heart skipped a beat. She was so lovely.

How did I get so lucky?

Harmony was smart, beautiful, and kind-hearted. Getting up the nerve to ask her out was the single best thing I'd ever done.

As soon as we hit the shadows, we collided like a hurricane. She jumped up, wrapping her legs around my waist, making me lose my mind in the process. I moved us against the wall for support. Her hands in my hair felt desperate. Our hips ground together, and she moaned softly.

It had been a while for us. I wanted her badly and it felt like the feeling was mutual. Suddenly, a bright light shone in our eyes and a deep male voice coughed loudly. Harmony shielded her eyes against the flashlight pointed at us.

I eased her down to the ground carefully and shoved my hands into my jeans to hide the obvious. Harmony straightened her skirt and adjusted her top before we filed out from behind the bleachers.

A sheriff's deputy lowered the light from our eyes and shook his head. "Aren't you two a little old to be doing this here?"

Harmony and I shared an embarrassed look, but I could tell she was on the verge of cracking up. "Yes, sir," we said in unison.

The deputy pointed toward the dance floor with his long black flashlight and we shuffled away before bursting into fits of laughter. We'd both been so busy that we hadn't had much time alone and it showed.

Seth came walking up to us with Cole in his wake. "I want to go home. I'm not feeling so good. Can you drive me to my car, so Cole can take me home?"

His face was pale, making his bruises stand out. "Maybe the celebration is a bit much since you just got out of the hospital. Sure, I'll take you." I turned to Harmony. "I'm sorry."

She smiled and patted Seth on the shoulder. "It's fine. I'm a bit tired myself. Sorry, you're not feeling well, Seth." She pulled her cell phone out of her back pocket. "I just need to make sure Lisa has a way home."

We walked out of the noisy gym and into the somewhat quieter night. The moon was full and bright. My head began to pound as we walked to my truck, so I guessed it was good that we were making an early evening of it. I must have shared that bug with Seth.

We drove my brothers to Seth's car that we'd left at the Walmart parking lot and waited while they got in.

"I'll take Harmony home and see you in a bit," I said, leaning out of the truck's window. They pulled out of the parking lot and I started to follow.

It was at that moment that I noticed movement at the back of the lot, where the lights hadn't worked for years.

Seven motorcycles were lined up, their drivers staring at us. I couldn't be sure, but I thought I recognized the leader. He appeared to be smiling.

My hands tightened on the steering wheel and my blood began to boil. I wanted to tear him apart for what he did to Seth. A gentle hand on my arm brought me out of my quickly rising rage.

"Liam, don't. They'll kill you. Let the sheriff handle it," she begged.

When I didn't answer or look away from the gang of bikers, she insisted. "Liam McKenzie, take me home—right now!"

That got my attention. I pulled my gaze from the bikers who had begun to get on their motorcycles, revving the engines loudly. The parking lot was mostly empty. I gave the leader one last long look, then pulled out of the parking lot and headed to Harmony's house.

I kept checking the rear-view mirror to make certain they hadn't followed us. The last thing I wanted was those psychos knowing where Harmony lived. When I was certain we hadn't been followed, I pulled up to Harmony's house, turned off the truck, and walked around to open her door.

Her street was lined with great oak trees that were so big their branches reached over the road and almost touched. It was one of the few residential streets that had the original street lights that also lined the sidewalks in downtown Summerset. All in all, it fit the ideal image of the perfect American postcard. So much so, the street was once featured in *Southern Living Magazine*.

Harmony stepped out of the truck and I could tell she was a bit shook up from seeing the bikers, or maybe my reaction to them. "I'm tired. You should call the sheriff."

"These guys keep slipping through their fingers and they're obviously not hiding. The sheriff's not going to do anything. And if they're really trying, they're pretty incompetent at their jobs." I was still amped-up from seeing them hanging out as nobody could touch them.

Were they waiting to jump one of us again? Were they hoping Seth would return to his car alone?

I tried to shake off the angry thoughts as I walked Harmony up to the sidewalk to her house.

As we approached the steps that led up to the front porch, I could barely make out a small dark mound in front of the door. It wasn't obvious what it was, but as we drew closer, I could see fur. Harmony screamed and darted for the steps before I knew what she was doing.

"Harmony, wait!" I said, rushing to catch her.

She dropped to her knees and began sobbing

uncontrollably as she hugged herself. I dropped down next to her and stared in shock. I reached for her and she buried her head in my chest. The front door opened, and Harmony's father looked down. "What the hell...?"

Harmony's calico cat, Sammy, was dead. From the look of it, the cat's throat had been cut right there on the porch. Without hesitating, Mr. Drake had his cell phone to his ear, calling the sheriff, no doubt.

I did the only thing I could do—I held Harmony while she sobbed her heart out. Mr. Drake must have come to the same conclusion. Someone did this on purpose. A piece of crumpled paper was lying next to Sammy. A small pool of blood threatened to reach it.

I picked it up to see what it was. There was one sentence, written on the back of a grocery store receipt in a messy hand. But that one sentence was powerful enough to make my stomach clench and my breath to catch.

Having any bad dreams, Liam?

Harmony was still crying against my chest. With a shaky hand, I passed the note to her father. He read it, and then looked at me for a long moment.

"Let's bring Harmony inside," he said, scanning the dark street.

I gathered Harmony in my arms and carried her inside to wait for the sheriff to arrive. Stepping over the poor animal, I wondered what kind of monster could do such a thing to a helpless creature?

CHAPTER
EIGHT

I woke to yelling in the house. It didn't take long to recognize Seth's voice, as I threw the covers back and ran out into the hall. Cole and Pa were right behind me, looking as sleepy and confused as I felt.

The yelling had stopped before we reached Seth's door. When I entered the room, I found Seth on the floor next to his bed, tangled in his sheets. He flinched when I entered and for a moment, didn't seem to recognize me. His face was white as a ghost and it looked like he may have been crying.

I approached him slowly and came to sit on the floor next to him. Seth looked more shook up than I'd ever seen him. "Seth, you okay?" I asked.

Pa and Cole seemed to understand that it was best not to smother him in his apparent state of mind. They hung back at the doorway and watched silently.

When Seth didn't answer me but sat there

breathing hard and staring at nothing, I asked again. "Seth. Are you all right? Was it a dream?"

He finally looked at me then and his eyes were haunted. "I guess." He looked around his room as if getting his bearings for the first time. "More like a nightmare I couldn't escape. It felt so real." Seth rubbed his hands over his face several times.

I put my hand on his shoulder. "Want to talk about it?" I'd had some terrible dreams over the last couple of months. The parts I could remember were too disturbing to share with anyone, so I'd kept the worst details to myself. *I wondered if Seth had a dream like that.*

Seth shook his head. I watched him closely. He seemed to be lost in his thoughts. "I'll be alright. Sorry to wake everyone. Was I talking in my sleep?" Seth asked, looking confused.

"More like yelling. Loud enough to wake the dead," Cole grumbled as he turned to leave. Pa stayed in the doorway, looking concerned.

I stood and reached my hand out to help Seth rise. He smiled weakly at me and took my hand. "Sorry, Pa." Seth sat on the edge of his bed and rested his elbows on his knees.

"No, bother. Everyone's had a bad dream at one point or another. I'll probably read a while in my room, Seth. If you have trouble falling back to sleep, come see me," Pa said.

He walked over and affectionately touched the top of Seth's head before leaving the room.

"When you're ready to talk about it, we can swap nightmares in the light of day—if you want." I stood and walked to the door.

"You still having those nightmares?" Seth asked.

"Yeah. More in the last couple of weeks. Seems like they've gotten worse." He nodded at me and I returned to my room. Morning would be just around the corner. I stretched out on the bed and stared at the cracks in the ceiling. My mind bounced between the ugly situation at Harmony's house and Seth's nightmare.

Harmony had been inconsolable, even yelling at the sheriff that if he didn't serve justice to those bikers, she would. It was an empty threat. Anyone who knew Harmony knew she wouldn't hurt a fly.

Her father was almost as vocal with the deputies that responded to his 911 call. His threats wouldn't have been empty. Her father was a decorated war hero, but he was careful enough in what he said to the authorities. But I saw the look in his eyes.

They knew where she lived, and they made certain I knew it. I understood their message, but I didn't understand why. Did they know something that I didn't? And now Seth was dreaming. Was there a connection, or was it just a bunch of random coincidences?

My life was beginning to feel more and more out of my control. Why this gang decided to zero in on me and everyone I know didn't make sense. They threatened me, then my family, and finally my future when they went after Harmony. There was something I was missing, but hell if I knew what it was. I hated feeling out of control.

There was one thing I could do. I could talk to

Pa about selling the farm. Win or lose, at least I had something I could work toward without feeling like my hands were tied.

I think we all must have slept late that morning. Pa was already gone when I finally drug myself into the kitchen. Coffee was ready, and I thanked God for that small blessing. Instead of the usual big breakfast, I made myself a big bowl of cereal and ate an orange. I was wiped out from the celebration and the emotional events from the previous night.

Cole, followed by Seth, entered the kitchen and ate the same as me. We mumbled our greetings, but nobody talked much through breakfast. When I finally told them I was going to talk to Pa about selling, they both agreed it was for the best. None of us had a strong desire to run the family farm, so there wasn't much reason to keep it.

I found Pa in the barn. He was wearing his big rubber boots over his work shoes. He rested his forearms on the wooden stockade inside the barn. He must have been catching his breath. I couldn't help but notice how very tired Pa seemed.

"Hey, Pa." I came to stand next to him as we watched the mama pig and her piglets running around her in the pen.

"Liam. I was just thinking about you. Feeling better?" he asked.

"Yeah, it comes and goes. I'm sure it's just a virus or something." Pa started walking through the barn to the back doors and I fell into step with him.

"Any more dreams?"

"Yes, sir," I said.

He studied me a moment. "I want you to make an appointment with Doc Harper. Just a check up to make sure we're not missing something," Pa said.

I wanted to argue that I'd be fine, but I simply nodded instead.

"Pa, I've been wanting to talk to you about something," I said.

Pa stopped and looked at me. "What is it, son?"

I wasn't certain how to begin the conversation I'd avoided for the last year.

"I think it's time to sell the farm, so you can retire." I watched his face closely for any signs that I'd upset him, but there were none.

Pa nodded his head. "Yes, you're right. I've been giving it a great deal of thought lately."

I stared at him, surprised by this reaction. "You have?"

He smiled then and grasped my shoulder. "I'm getting too old for this life and farming just isn't what my boys are called to do, and that's all right. It was a good living for my father and me. And it was a good place to raise three rambunctious boys." Pa squeezed my shoulder, then started walking toward the tractor. I followed him, still shocked by how easy this had been.

"You're not sad about giving it up? When you didn't bring it up, I thought maybe you needed this to keep busy. You know after Ma left." I looked up at him seated on the tractor.

"I didn't bring it up because I was worried that it was too much for you boys to lose your ma and have so many changes happen right afterward," Pa said smiling. "I guess we were both worried about each other."

He winked at me and started the tractor. I watched as he drove around the barn and out of sight. I walked back through the barn on my way toward the house.

I couldn't believe it. It was all going to work. Seth would play college football, I'd move to California with Harmony, and Cole would have an ordinary high school experience without the added stress of running the farm. And Pa would finally get the rest he deserved.

I visualized him meeting the other retired men in town to drink coffee and argue politics. Maybe he'd fish more and learn how to use the computer we bought for him and Ma two years ago. Ma had learned how to use email, but I don't think Pa ever touched the thing.

I needed to see Harmony. Maybe my news would help lift her spirits. She hadn't returned my calls, but I knew she was still in shock about what had happened and that she'd be mourning the loss of Sammy for a long time.

When I arrived at Harmony' front door, I could see that the blood had been washed away. It felt surreal in the light of day as if it had never happened.

Mrs. Drake, who resembled her daughter in many ways, welcomed me into their home. "She's in her room. Maybe you can get her to talk. I don't blame her one bit, but I've never seen her this upset. I've made some sweet tea. Would you like some?" she asked.

"No, ma'am. But thank you."

She nodded, and I went up the stairs. Harmony's door was the last one at the end of the hall on the left. After knocking softly, I eased the door open cautiously.

The shades were drawn, making the room dark. Tiny blue lights were hung around her window. The room was very feminine and hadn't changed since high school. Harmony was under the covers of her bed, with her face resting on a pillow.

Her eyes were red and swollen, and her hair was a mess. I sat on the edge of the bed next to her and moved some of the strands away from her tear-stained face. "I'm so sorry, Harmony."

"I know," she said. Her hand came out of the covers to find mine and she held it close to her face.

"I have some news that might help," I said.

She reached for a tissue from the nightstand and dabbed at her face before sitting up in bed. "What is it?"

"Pa's going to sell. I spoke with him today and he agreed."

She blinked at me several times like this was

the last thing she expected to hear. "Are you serious?"

"Would I tease about something like this?"

Her face broke into a wide smile and my heart soared. It killed me to see her upset, and to know that I was somehow responsible was even worse.

She threw her arms around me and squealed happily. A moment later her mother opened the door in a panic. "What's—?" She stopped when she saw her daughter's smile. Her mom exhaled dramatically and then smiled. "I wish you'd have stopped by hours ago, Liam." She closed the door without another word.

Harmony and I looked at one another. "I can't tell you how happy this makes me, Liam. There's no pressure. We'll just see where it all leads, okay?" she said, looking hopeful.

"Agreed. No pressure, but you're not allowed to dump me for a surfer dude, ever," I teased, before leaning in to kiss her softly. I pulled away and she sank back into the pillows.

"I'm not making any promises I might not be able to keep," she said, winking at me. She looked toward the window. "Do you mind opening that for me? I think I'm ready for some sunshine now."

I did as she asked, and the room flooded with filtered sunlight. I returned to the bed and sat again.

"Better?" I asked.

"Much," she said. Her smile faltered as she stared out the window. "Poor Sammy. I hope he didn't suffer. I hope—" She couldn't seem to finish. She shook her head as if denying the thoughts.

I gathered her into my arms. "Do you think I'm a bad person, Liam?" she asked in a muffled voice, her face against my shoulder.

I pulled her away so I could see her face. "Never. Why would you ask me that?"

Her eyes filled with new tears. "Because I hate them for what they did, and I even wished them dead. I've never wished anything so awful on another person. And the worst part…I can't take it back. I'm trying to forgive them. I know it's the Christian thing to do, but I can't bring myself to do it. And it makes me feel bad about myself." She looked away.

I knew exactly how she felt. But in my dreams, I'd done more than wish bad things on them. I'd acted on those feelings.

"It's perfectly normal for you to feel this way. It was only last night. I can't say that I haven't wished the same thing, Harmony. You're not a bad person. You're human." She smiled through her tears and nodded her head repeatedly as if she needed to hear it. Just to know that one tragedy hadn't tarnished her soul in some way.

"Thank you." She fell back onto the pillow and her eyes seemed heavy. "If you don't mind, I think I can sleep now. It was a rough night with little rest."

"Of course. Want me to close the blinds again?"

Her eyes were already closed. "No, leave them. I don't want to be in the dark anymore."

I kissed the top of her head and quietly let myself out.

CHAPTER
NINE

PA WAS WATCHING a news channel in the living room and Cole was on the couch, filling out an application for the new Super Store that was opening next month. Seth and I were in charge of dinner that night, so we were busy in the kitchen.

I was feeling pretty good about everything except the handful of question marks floating around my head. What happened to our mother and when was the best time to talk to my brothers about what I'd learned? It wasn't happy news, so I felt it could wait a bit longer, considering what had transpired this past week. We'd had enough drama.

Seth and I placed the food on the kitchen table and called Pa and Cole to dinner. Pa had just switched the TV off when a call came through on his cell phone. We sat at the table and waited for him to join us. We always said grace before the evening meal.

After a couple of minutes, Pa walked into the kitchen, looking grim. He sat down heavily and looked at each one of us in turn. Finally, he rested his gaze on me.

"That was the sheriff calling. They caught that guy who threatened you. Harmony identified him. His name is Alistair Wilson."

"What? Where is she?" I demanded, jumping up from the table.

Pa motioned for me to sit down, but I hesitated. "She's fine, son. He never even knew she was there. She was behind a one-way mirror. The sheriff said she's mighty shook up and I'm sure you'll want to go see her after dinner, but we have some things to talk about as a family, right?"

I returned to my seat. "What's his story? Who is he?" I asked, loading mashed potatoes onto my plate and then passing the bowl to Cole.

"Turns out he's wanted for questioning in connection with two different homicides. One in Pennsylvania, and one in Alabama. The sheriff said he's considered a person of interest, but he has a record a mile long." Pa took a moment to chew his food.

"Sounds like we're lucky Seth's alive," I said, considering the implications.

"He's wanted for murder?" Cole asked as if he couldn't wrap his mind around the notion that a murderer was here in Summerset.

"We don't know that, but the idea that he's associated in some way with two different murders does throw some serious suspicion on the man," Pa said.

"And after what he did to Harmony's cat, I wouldn't put it past him," I said, still angry but relieved he was behind bars and would face justice.

"Sheriff said the FBI is flying down tomorrow to question him and possibly start procedures to extradite him back to Pennsylvania, depending on how the interrogation goes."

We sat eating in silence for a few minutes.

"Seth, you're lucky to be alive. And Liam, he threatened to kill you. And what about that note he left for you? What the hell you think that was about?" Cole asked while going for seconds on the roast beef.

Seth had been quiet throughout the conversation. Something was up with my normally care-free, devil-may-care brother. He seemed preoccupied all day. I was trying to give him space, but he had me worried.

"Shall we talk about the farm?" Pa asked, seeming to know the conversation needed a new direction. We nodded.

"I called Fred Pettersen after talking with each of you today. He's willing to put the farm on the market for us. There's no telling how long it will take, but I don't expect it to be a quick process. I'm going to start selling off the livestock as soon as possible. How do you boys feel about that?" Pa asked, leaning back in his chair and taking a sip of coffee. Pa drank coffee with every meal.

"That's fast," Seth said.

"Yes, but if you're all ready, I agree it's the next step. You're leaving in four weeks for college. You'll be gone before the farm is, Seth. What's troubling you, son?"

Seth looked annoyed with the attention. "Where will you live?"

Pa looked surprised by the question. "I'll be right here. I'm not selling the house or barn, and I'll keep five acres for myself. I want to get your ma's garden growing again. It'll give me something to do," he said smiling.

"So, I get to stay here, with no chores?" Cole asked excitedly.

Pa laughed. "You'll still have chores, just not the same ones." Cole's expression slumped, and I reached over and tousled his hair until he swatted my hand away.

Pa looked at me a moment. "What will you do, Liam?"

I had the sneaking suspicion that Pa already knew about my plans to leave.

All their attention was on me, and I somehow felt guilty. "I thought I'd go to California with Harmony. I can see if the fire departments are hiring and maybe start some classes at one of the community colleges to start." Cole and Seth blinked at me.

"Woohoo! I knew it! You're going to marry Harmony," Cole said with way too much enthusiasm.

Seth just stared at me like I'd betrayed him or something. "I guess we'll be about as far away from each other as possible. Me in Pitt, and you all the way across the country." Seth got up from the table and took his dishes to the sink, then started cleaning up.

"It's not like it's forever, Seth. We'll all come home for the holidays or as often as possible," I said, getting up to help him.

Seth ignored me as he continued to fill the sink with soapy water.

"Seth, what's wrong?" I asked, unsure why I'd upset him.

Seth glared at me then and threw the rag into the water, sending suds and water everywhere. "Everything, Liam." He turned and stormed out of the kitchen.

I looked at Cole and Pa. Cole shrugged his shoulders and got up to help me finish cleaning up.

"Just give him some space. Seth's not as immune to change as he wants everyone to think. Most likely, he thinks he'll lose his family through all these changes. And sometimes I believe Ma's passing affected him the most," Pa said as he stood to leave.

"I thought Seth handled it better than any of us. He kept it together when Liam and I lost it, time and again," Cole said, as he dried a plate and put it away.

"That's exactly what I mean," Pa said as he turned to leave. "He didn't allow himself to grieve like we did."

I thought about that for a moment. Could he be right about Seth? It did seem like he was so much stronger than the rest of us. He kept his chin up and the rest of us moving. I never gave it much thought, although I was a bit envious since I was the oldest and felt it should have been me comforting the family and making arrangements.

His crazy antics had us smiling and laughing only weeks after her passing. Was it all a front to avoid facing the pain?

I called Harmony after dinner, and she told me how awful it had been to look at the man who had so viciously killed her cat, Sammy. She said she was certain he could see her, even though the sheriff tried to assure her that Alistair couldn't see through the glass.

At one point, Harmony said he pointed right at her through the mirror, and said, 'Tell Liam I'm coming for him and the rest of his pack.' Understandably, that shook her up. And since the rest of his gang was still at large, her father was keeping her under lock and key, meaning no visitors, which included me.

We had eaten dinner late, so it was no surprise that we were all still hanging out in the living room watching a *Star Wars* movie at half past midnight. Pa had fallen asleep in his recliner and was snoring softly. The movie was close to ending when Pa's phone rang. The ringing startled him awake and he answered it right away.

Phone calls in the middle of the night never came with good news. Seth, who had joined us shortly after the movie started, now turned the volume down. Cole, Seth, and I listened intently.

"Hello?"

There was silence as we waited and listened.

"Good, lord," Pa said. "How long ago?" He was already getting out of his chair. "Appreciate you letting me know. I will. Goodbye." He ended the call. Pa's face looked pale.

Sensing something was wrong, Seth and I stood when Pa did.

"What is it? What happened?" I asked.

Pa looked at me, concern in his tired eyes. "Alistair Wilson murdered a deputy while escaping from county jail tonight."

I felt the blood drain from my face and suddenly there wasn't enough oxygen in the room. None of us said a word. I quickly texted Harmony what had happened in case she hadn't heard and slipped the phone in my pocket.

"Should we be worried?" Cole asked nervously.

"I'm sure they're trying to get as far away from Summerset as possible. He won't waste time on Liam or whatever imagined grudge he's holding. But just to be safe, the Sheriff's sending a couple of deputies to watch our place tonight. Simply a precaution because he's made threats toward Liam and his family."

Pa's words were meant to comfort us, but I could tell he wasn't taking this lightly. "I'll go make some coffee for those deputies. They'll be here in thirty to forty minutes. You boys get to bed."

Pa went into the kitchen to make the coffee but Seth, Cole, and I just stared at each other. That's when we heard it.

Several vehicles were coming up the long dirt drive toward the house. Seth looked at me. It was too soon for the sheriff's deputies to assemble and make it out to our house. And from the sound of the engines, they were motorcycles.

TEN

I RAN to the front door and threw it open, only to be blinded by multiple bright headlights shining on me. Multiple engines revved loudly, and I held a hand up to shield my eyes.

Seth and Cole came to stand on either side of me. Even when the engines died, the lights stayed on, so that all we could see were dark silhouettes as the riders got off their motorcycles and came to stand in front of them. I noticed two of the forms appeared to be women.

"What do you want?" I yelled.

"You know what we want. I think I was pretty clear about that at the diner, *Liam*," said the now familiar voice of the Alastair Wilson. "Is this the extent of your pack? Just the three of you?" he asked.

Again, with the 'pack' reference. *Was that a term bikers used for gang?*

"You need to get off our land now. Sheriff is on his way. We don't want any trouble," I said, taking a few steps down the porch. I sensed rather than saw my brothers move with me, as if we were thinking and acting as one.

"You're not as smart as you look, are you, kid? Are your brothers as ready to die as you? Maybe they'd rather join us, over the alternative."

Cole and Seth remained silent. Knowing he'd murdered a guard just this evening made me fear for the safety of my family—but I knew that I'd die to protect them.

"Well, it's settled then. If it's a bloodbath you want, that's what you'll get." The entire group began moving toward the porch and once again, that sick feeling in my gut returned. I could feel perspiration break out all over my body. Just like that, I felt feverish.

My hands fisted tightly at my sides, trying to force myself to stay calm and fight the ill feeling rising in me.

In the dimness of the night, I saw their eyes glow amber. This wasn't a trick of the light, and it scared the hell out of me. Cole and Seth must have seen the same, because we all stumbled backwards to get back onto the porch, quickly.

"What the hell—?" Seth breathed.

"Liam?" Cole's voice was shaky.

They kept coming, slow and sure. It was their menacing pace, and their glowing eyes that made the scene feel unreal and totally wrong—a waking nightmare. The cramping in my gut grew worse and I almost doubled over.

From the side of the yard, the sound of a shotgun being cocked turned every head, including mine. Alistair and his gang momentarily halted their advance.

Pa stood in the yard with a shotgun pointed toward Alistair. "You folks best get back on those bikes of yours and get off my land. I won't tell you twice." He must have come from the back of the house.

My mind went through all the ways this could go wrong, but I never expected what happened next.

"Pa," Cole said, sounding frightened.

"Go on into the house, Cole. The sheriff and his deputies are on their way," Pa said.

In the next second, one of the gang members moved. Another second and the gun went off, but the shot went up into the air as the large man snatched it out of Pa's hands, sending him flailing backward onto the ground.

"Pa!" our voices cried as one.

Cole leaped over the porch wall, landing on the grass, and sprinted toward our father. The man who had moved impossibly fast stepped into Cole's path, preventing him from reaching Pa. The guy tossed the shotgun to the ground and stalked toward Cole.

That's when the pain in my body became unbearable. I screamed and dropped to my knees. I was so hot, it felt like I was on fire. I had to get my clothes off. I kicked off my boots and pulled my t-shirt over my head.

"What are you doing?" Seth demanded, panic making his voice rise.

"What he was born to do, boy," the leader said,

laughing. "It's what he is. It's what you all are."
His mocking laughter sounded like nails on a
chalkboard in my head.

At that moment, the man shoved Cole down
when he tried once again to reach Pa, who was still
lying on the ground, looking dazed.

When I looked at the leader again, a great
black wolf stood in his place. Beside him was a
pile of empty clothing. The wolf growled and
stalked toward the porch.

"Holy sh—!" Seth tried to say.

Everything in my vision went red. My body
suddenly felt free, like a weight had been lifted.
And with it, my focus sharpened and zeroed in on
the black wolf. The wolf stopped and the fur on his
back stood on end. I didn't hesitate. I launched myself at the black wolf.

I could hear familiar voices calling my name,
but I couldn't make sense of it anymore. The wolf
and I collided in mid-air and then crashed and
rolled across the grass. We were back on our feet
within seconds, circling each other like the animals
we were.

Growling and jaws snapping in warning and
fear—*his, not mine*. I smelled the fear of my
enemy.

A voice caught my attention for a second.
"Pa!" I looked in the direction of the cry. One of
my pack was holding the other. While I tried to understand why the younger one was upset, the black
wolf attacked.

He went for my throat but missed. When he
pulled back for another try, I clamped my jaws

down tight on his throat and refused to let go. A feeling of familiarity came over me—a dream.

Growls and howling from the others did not hinder my attack. They wouldn't interfere. I was challenging their Alpha. If I won, they would follow me or run away. If I lost, they'd kill my pack after I'm dead. But I would never let that happen.

With a renewed determination, I bit down hard until I felt and heard a snap. Instantly, the black wolf stopped struggling and laid still. Crying and screaming came from the shocked females, quiet growls from the others. I looked down at my kill. A man laid at my feet, death shining in his glossy stare.

A voice I'd thought long gone screamed in my head, 'What have you done?' I backed away from the body, confused. Why was this wrong? I looked to my right and another dark wolf stood beside me. He's part of my pack, but I smelled fear on him. Were we still in danger?

I looked at the boy holding the old man in his arms. He stared at me in terror as he rocked the old man's limp body. He's gone—the old man. That pained me for some reason—aw, yes. He's pack too. That meant something. I tried to protect him but failed.

Far away, I heard sirens. The others heard it too. They gathered the body and clothes of the black wolf. One carried him into the forest and the others hurriedly got on their metal beasts and rode away. They continued to look over their shoulders fearfully until they put some distance between us.

I felt that I should stay to protect the younger one, but I knew the sound meant danger. I looked at the boy who stared at me with tears running down his face. He still held our fallen in his arms.

Moving closer to him, I whimpered to let him know I was sorry. He hesitantly reached a hand out to touch me but became frightened and stopped before he did.

I turned away and trotted off into the forest. The other wolf would follow, so I began to run.

The moon was calling.

CHAPTER
ELEVEN

THE GROUND WAS damp beneath me, and the air was thick and cool. This would have been a comfortable temperature if I wasn't covered in dew and...naked.

Leaves, twigs, and rocks pressed into my backside as I laid there staring at the branches of the trees overhead. In the early morning, just before the sun showed itself in the sky, the forest would have felt peaceful, if it wasn't so very wrong that I was there. Had it all been another nightmare?

Lord, let it be a bad dream, I prayed.

My mind tried to put the pieces together but there were gaps, along with blurry flashes of images that made it difficult. In that way, it was much like a dream.

The muscles in my body ached as if I'd run a marathon. When I looked to my right, I saw Seth curled on his side, sleeping. I knew he was by the steady way his chest rose and fell. He too was naked.

I pushed up to a seated position and looked

around, trying to determine our location. My movements must have woken Seth. He jumped up so fast that I flinched in surprise. He looked frantically around the forest and then at me.

The disturbed look on his face made me embarrassed for both of us. We got to our feet and started brushing off leaves and dirt. Not that it mattered. We were stark naked in the middle of the woods. I had a pretty good idea where we were. At least we were still on our land.

"What happened to us, Liam?" Seth asked, his voice thick with emotion.

"I don't know, but we need to get back to Pa and Cole. We'll sort the rest out then. Pa will know what to do." But then I remembered something from the night before. I looked at Seth and we both must have had the same thought.

I began to run for home, praying that my disjointed memories were wrong. Seth followed close behind me. The pain in my bare feet and our obvious nudity was forgotten. Getting home was the only thing that mattered to me.

We were pretty far from the house and our run turned into a jog after ten minutes or so. It still took us a while to reach the field closest to the house. I remembered coming through this exact area last night. After that, I didn't remember much until I woke that morning.

I was horrified at the flashes of memories of

what I did. Or, what I thought I did. *Was I a monster? Was Seth?*

Those questions would have to wait. I needed to know that Pa and Cole were safe. I'd deal with the consequences of my actions later.

We reached the wire fence that kept the cattle out of that field until we were ready to let them graze there. On two different wooden posts were small bundles of clothes, shoes, cell phones, and a hand-written note from Cole.

It read *It's safe to come home. Cole.*

We dressed hastily and made our way anxiously through the tall grass. Cole was sitting on the front porch with a cup of coffee in his hand, watching us approach. He no longer had the fear that I saw in his eyes when he looked at me.

All I saw was pain. Deep in my soul, I knew what he had to tell us, and I so badly wanted to run back into the woods, so that I'd never had to hear it.

Cole's eyes were red and swollen. He looked us over closely as if confirming we were indeed his brothers and not the creatures that went into the woods last night.

Cole put his cup on the ground and stood. He walked over to us and threw his arms around Seth and me. He hadn't said a word, but the tears came anyway. Seth cried silently but his body shook from the effort. We stayed like that for a long time.

Eventually, we silently followed Cole inside and sat at the kitchen table together. At first, nobody spoke. It's as if there were too much to put into words. We all had many questions and no answers.

Feeling overwhelmed and small, I stared at Pa's chair, wishing he were there to guide us through what to do next. I didn't want to hear it, but I needed to know what happened. I was the first to break the silence. "He's gone, isn't he?" I could barely get the words out.

Cole didn't speak. He just nodded his head and looked like he was trying to hold back his emotions. Seth put his head on the table and cried more silent tears. I put my hand on his shoulder.

"What happened...after we left?" I asked.

Cole cleared his throat and wiped his eyes with his t-shirt. "He died in my arms before you left, I think. I hid the last two bikes in the barn before the sheriff got here. I was afraid they'd ask questions I couldn't answer." Cole looked at us. "I was so afraid that nobody would believe me, and if they did, they might hunt you both or put you in jail for killing that guy." Cole looked down at his coffee cup like he had the weight of the world on his shoulders. That night, he did.

I grasped his hand and squeezed it. "You didn't do anything wrong, Cole. I did. You just tried to protect me. None of this is your fault. I know if Pa were here...he'd be proud of the way you handled yourself."

"What happened to you both? One minute you were you and then you were..." Cole trailed off. "How the hell is that shit even possible?"

"I don't know what happened to Seth or me, or why. It frightened us too," I offered.

"I've never been so scared in my life," Seth said, raising his head. "It was like a living nightmare I couldn't wake from." He ran his fingers through his dark hair.

"The sheriff let me stay here last night, but just barely. I told him you and Seth were camping, but you'd be home early this morning. I insisted on being the one to tell you. He finally agreed when I showed him Pa's guns and convinced him I knew how to use them. I've been waiting for you to come back ever since," Cole said. "I'm glad you came back. I wasn't certain you would or could come back."

"What are we going to do?" Seth asked.

They both looked at me. I realized there and then that they were depending on me to take up where Pa left off. Those were shoes I'd never come close to filling. "We can't tell anyone about this. They'd think we were crazy and maybe lock us up." I got up and poured another cup of black coffee, then returned to my seat. "I know that's exactly what I'd think if someone told me what they saw last night."

"What about the others? I think they're like… us. What if they come for us again?" Seth asked. Nobody answered for a moment.

"We won't be here if they do," I said.

Seth and Cole looked at me strangely. "Where would we go?" asked Cole.

"It doesn't matter. We can go anywhere, as long as they can't find us," Seth added, his mind already speeding along. He seemed to have gotten ahold of himself and that intelligent brain of his was kicking into gear. That was a good thing. He needed a distraction. We all did. Thinking about Pa was crippling, and we needed to move fast.

"Seth's right. Start thinking about where you'd like to live and why it's the best choice. We'll decide that last. First, we have to take care of matters with the farm and…" I couldn't even say the word *burial*.

My eyes threatened to tear, but I fought it down and covered it with a cough. They needed me to be strong. It was the least I could do.

"Liam?" Cole asked in a cautious tone.

"Yeah?"

"Will that happen to me?" Cole's face was full of fear and I didn't blame him one bit.

"I don't know, Cole. I don't know why it happened to me or Seth. But if it does, we'll be there for you. You won't be alone, ever." I put my hand over his. Cole gave me a nervous smile that failed to reach his eyes.

I'd been wondering the same thing. Was it a virus? Did I give it to Seth? I was at a loss, with no idea where to look for answers. So, I focused on the one thing I could do for now. I would protect my family. We'd sell the farm to the first decent offer. I figured that would be the Coopers.

The Cooper farm butted up against ours to the east and Old Man Cooper had been harping on Pa to sell him part of his land for years. Now he'd get his chance.

I called the sheriff to let him know we'd made it back and had heard the sad news. He offered his condolences. Pa had been a friend of his for many years.

It wasn't any time before word spread and the good people of Summerset began showing up at our door with enough food to feed an army. There were people coming and going most of the day. We ran out of room in the fridge and had to put some things in the freezer.

Later that day, I had to *officially* identify my father. The sheriff said it was a technicality, but one we had to do. Seth and Cole didn't want to go. On the drive over, I began to wonder about how he died.

What brought on the heart attack? Was it being knocked to the ground, or was it what he saw? Did seeing me turn into a monster kill him?

If I allowed myself to dwell on that, I'd be of no use to anyone, so I pushed that thought someplace deep in my mind where the sun doesn't shine. When we were safe, I'd visit the idea some more.

The coroner pulled back a white sheet to reveal my father's body. I nodded my head and wiped at my eyes for the hundredth time that day. They told me he died of a massive heart attack.

When they asked if I'd like a moment alone with him, I said that I would. The coroner and the sheriff left the room, and I stood next to his body and cried some more.

After a few minutes, I said, "Pa, I don't know if

you can hear me all the way from Heaven, but I want you to know how sorry I am about what…I am. And what I did." I paused to compose myself. It was important to me that I say this to him.

"I promise you this, I'll watch over Cole and Seth with my very life. You can count on that." I wiped my eyes so that I could see.

"Tell Mama hello and give her a kiss from me." With that, I turned and walked out of the sterile white room and never looked back.

Pa wouldn't want us to hold onto ghosts, just good memories. Thanks to two kind-hearted people, my brothers and I had loads of good memories to carry us through.

When I returned home, Harmony was sitting on the front porch with Cole and Seth. I could tell she'd been crying. The boys looked beat up and tired.

She rushed down the steps and threw herself into my arms. I held her tightly. We stayed that way for a long while.

Seth and Cole must have gone inside, leaving us alone when we walked up to the porch. We sat in the swing silently. Harmony cried the only evidence was her sniffles. She held my hand and we rocked gently.

Eventually, her crying stopped, and she rested her head on my shoulder. It gave me peace to be there with her and imagine a life with her by my side. Even if only for a moment.

Harmony finally broke the silence. "I wanted to come first thing, but with the murderer on the loose, my daddy wouldn't let me out of his sight. I had to sneak out to come when I did." She gently turned my face toward her. "Are you okay?"

I looked into her gentle face and wanted desperately to share the whole ugly secret with her. *What would she say? What would she think?*

I wanted to tell her she had nothing to fear from Alistair Wilson. He wouldn't be bothering anyone ever again. At least I hoped our…*kind* didn't come back from death. "I'll be okay, Harmony. We'll be alright."

There was no way I was bringing Harmony into this. I didn't even know what *this* was. The only certainty was that not knowing put us in danger from others like us, and I couldn't tell anyone about it.

How do you win the game when you don't know the rules? There was no one we could reach out to for help. We'd have to figure this out on our own, in our own time.

We were alone, but we had each other.

CHAPTER
TWELVE

It was the morning of the funeral, and I knew I had to tell my brothers about our mother. They had a right to know, and as it stood, there would never be a right time to share such news. I didn't feel right withholding it any longer. Certainly, after what happened to Seth and me, I was certain it was related in some way.

We'd cleaned up after breakfast and had finished the chores around the farm that couldn't be ignored, even for a funeral.

For some reason, we were ready early. We wore the suits Ma had insisted we have for the church, weddings, and funerals. I'd worn it two times too many in the last year.

"I need to tell you something that Pa shared with me just before he passed. I was hoping there'd be a better time to talk about it, but…"

We were sitting on the front porch, talking about funny things Pa used to do or say. It felt good to remember things that made us laugh, even if it was bittersweet.

Ma would have loved this. She always made a big fuss when her boys got all dressed up. And every time, she'd have to pull out the little camera we gave her for Christmas one year. I wondered if Cole and Seth were remembering the same thing.

"Tell us," Seth said.

I told them everything Pa had told me about our mother being found dead in a remote part of the woods in Tennessee. I showed them the picture of her wolf tattoo, which took on a whole new meaning now. And I told them how we were found with her, malnourished, dehydrated, but otherwise unharmed.

Was our mother like us? Was she murdered because of it? Or was she truly killed by an unidentified animal, as they suspected? Couldn't a wolf be that animal?

Just like I had, they had many questions. We still knew so little about where we came from or what we were. I'd researched the news stories online, but it was all the same—one mysterious death and three survivors. None of us had any memories of what had happened to our mother or why we were left in the woods.

One thing was certain if someone did murder our mother, they were cold-blooded enough to leave three defenseless children alone in the woods to die. *What would that person do if they realized we had survived? Did they already know?*

By this time, we had no more tears left to cry for the mother we didn't remember. Maybe someday we'd return to that place and give her a proper farewell. I was sad that I couldn't remember her. I was almost seven when we were adopted. Why couldn't I remember? Was it so traumatic that my mind refused to go back?

The funeral service was nice. Many people gave speeches about how Pa had helped them in one way or another. Some others he gave of his time or loaned his equipment. He was a generous man and well-loved by his community.

The rest of the funeral was a blur and exhausting. There was a reception at the church gym and it was packed. The Ladies' Quilting Club that Ma had belonged to, organized the celebration of life gathering and handled all the details, for which I was thankful.

Old Man Cooper came to share his condolences and I brought up that we were selling the farm. He looked conflicted, discussing the sale on the day of the funeral, but I explained we were leaving soon to get Seth settled into college and wanted to have it started before we did.

He seemed to accept this explanation and we agreed on a fair price. I also used this opportunity to speak to the ladies in the quilting club about running an estate sale of items in the house that we weren't taking with us—which was mostly everything.

They were surprised but pleased when I told them the money could go toward the charity of their choosing, as long as it served the community of Summerset. Cole, Seth, and I felt it was fitting, and that Ma and Pa would have supported our decision. We had more than enough money to live off, pay for college, and beyond.

Harmony hovered close to me the entire day, but I made certain she was not nearby when I discussed our leaving. I wanted to tell her alone. As far as she knew, we were still moving to California together. The news would hurt her and me.

By the end of the day, I still couldn't bring myself to confess. Maybe leaving was the best way to break the news. There was nothing I could say to make it better. She'd view it as rejection no matter what I said. And it wasn't like we could let anyone know where to find us. I had to end it completely, for her own good.

Maybe if she hated me, it would be easier to move on for both of us.

———

The sale of the farm was substantial. Pa had the foresight to set up a living trust and had named me as the executor. We didn't need to go to court for several years in order to execute a will.

I had instant power-of-attorney and could liquidate the estate as needed.

Seth and I were loading up some of the livestock that we'd sold when Cole came running into the barn.

"I know where we can move to," he said with some of his old enthusiasm.

"Where?" I asked, grinning at Seth.

"There's this town up in the mountains of Arizona. There's a college there, but it's not too big. There's the forest and lots of lands. I figured a big city is out of the question since hair and fangs don't go over well there." I looked at Seth and we both started laughing at Cole's joke. It actually made me feel more normal to laugh about it. At least for the moment. And, it felt good to laugh with my brothers again.

"Yep, no big cities for sure," I said.

"So what's this town called?" Seth asked.

"Flagstaff. Seth can go to college there. They even have a football team—division one, I believe. And, it even has its own fire department, not volunteer. I know you'll be interested in that, Liam," Cole said, going for the hard sell.

"What about the high school? Have you checked into that?" I asked.

"Sure have. I even started the online registration process. You can finish it since you're my legal guardian now." The reality of that hit home and we just stood looking at one another.

"All right, Cole. What else you got?" I asked. Cole seemed to be in a better place, having something to focus on.

"I'm not going to college anymore," Seth said.

"What? Why?" I asked, not liking his change in direction.

"I just don't want to."

"Just because you're not taking the scholarship, doesn't mean you can't go to school. We've got plenty of money for that." I stopped working and watched him.

Seth continued to load bags of feed into the

back of Pa's pickup that we'd backed into the barn. "It's not important to me anymore, that's all."

Cole and I shared a look. "Why? Just tell me why," I said.

Seth stopped what he was doing and wiped the sweat from his forehead. "Because I was only going to college for Pa. It was his dream for me, not mine. It was never mine. I just wanted to make him happy, but he's gone."

I never realized that Seth didn't want to go to college. "But you love football and you're so stinking smart. Why wouldn't you?"

He looked at me like I was ignorant, then gave me one of those cocky grins he was well-known for. "Liam, I don't like football. I just happened to be good at it, and everyone, including you, assumed I loved to play." Seth took off his gloves and ran his hands through his hair. "I like to watch some football while drinking a beer. I enjoy dating cheerleaders. And, I really…loved when Ma's and Pa's faces lit up when I was offered that scholarship." His mood changed from teasing to serious with a single look.

"And I'd go all the way for a doctorate to see that look again, but they're not here anymore," Seth said. We just stared at one another.

"I'm sorry. I'm sorry that I didn't see this. I should have known. I'm your brother. That's my job," I said.

He nodded. "It's okay. I won't take your *brother of the year* award from you. You can keep the trophy." He winked, then looked at his watch.

"Damn, I got to go," Seth said, turning to jog toward the house.

"We're not done!" I yelled, after him.

"Cole can finish. He's obviously got nothing better to do," he said.

"I'm working," Cole complained.

"I've got a date. Last chance to dance with a Summerset girl," Seth yelled over his shoulder.

"I didn't hear about any dance," Cole said, scratching his head.

"Pretty sure that was code for something else that doesn't have anything to do with dancing," I said, shaking my head.

"Oh," Cole said, drawing out the word.

Some things never changed.

CHAPTER

THIRTEEN

ALL THE FARM equipment was sold off quickly. Our neighbor decided to buy the land next to his and promised to find a buyer for the rest by working through the local realtor and lawyer we'd hired from New York City to handle our affairs.

"Why'd you hire a fancy lawyer from New York City?" Seth had asked.

"We don't want anyone to trace us when we leave. If we used someone local, or even one of the neighboring cities, there's always a chance they could know us or someone we know. All our money will go through him so nobody can track us that way," I said.

"Did he ask any questions about why we didn't want to be found?" Seth wanted to know.

"He must have other clients with the same demands because he never blinked an eye. He even gave me the contacts and information on using aliases, and details on how to stay under the radar. I'm still reading through it all," I said. Seth seemed satisfied with my reasoning, if not impressed.

When the day of the estate sale came, we had Pa's truck packed full of our personal belongings and a few things we couldn't bring ourselves to part with —Pa's worn recliner and Ma's wicker rocking chair. She'd painstakingly restored the antique chair and would sit and watch the sun setting or rising with a glass of iced tea or a cup of coffee, depending on the time.

None of us wanted to part with the chairs, so we packed them in the truck with our camping gear, duffle bags, and backpacks. We each took a couple of small personal items that reminded us of our parents.

I took Pa's pipe and tobacco, and a small framed picture of him and Ma. Cole took one of the photo albums and an old John Deere cap that Pa wore daily. It was frayed and stained from hard work.

Seth came out of the house with a small shoe box tucked under his arm. He didn't volunteer what he'd kept, and Cole and I didn't ask.

People were arriving, and many were leaving with bits and pieces of our family's lives. It was difficult to watch, and we hadn't planned to stay as long as we had.

The ladies from Ma's old quilting club were organized and efficient, as piece by piece our world was sold to the highest bidder, quickly becoming absorbed into other people's lives.

Mrs. Harper, a short thick woman with blue-tinted hair came to me and hugged me around my waist briefly. "It breaks my heart to see your parents possessions sold off, but I do believe you're right to do it. How are you boys holding up?" she asked.

"We're doing all right. Thank you for handling all of this. We wouldn't have known the first thing about having an estate sale. You and the other ladies are a godsend," I said.

"I see you have the truck loaded, are you leaving already?" she asked as Cole and Seth walked up to us, carrying a few last-minute supplies for the road.

"Yes, ma'am. We're going early to get Seth settled in before school starts next month," I lied.

Cole raised his eyebrows at me.

"That's a shame, but as long as you boys have each other, I'm confident you'll be just fine. So, it's Pittsburgh that you're headed to?" Mrs. Harper asked.

"Yes, ma'am. Cole and I will so that we can all stay together for a while," I said, feeling bad about lying to her.

"Well, leave me your address, so we can keep tabs on you boys," she said.

I handed her a business card.

"Here's the card for the lawyer who will be handling the estate, if you have any questions or if you should need to reach us, he'll know how to get ahold of us." She looked confused but nodded her head. She smiled at us and gathered Cole and Seth into a quick group hug.

"Take care of one another. Family is every-thing," she said, then returned to her work.

"You're going to hell for lying to Mrs. Harper. You know that, right?" Seth teased.

"Shut up. I feel bad enough. Can't be helped," I replied.

"I sorta feel like we're going undercover, like the Bond brothers, or something," Cole said, and we all laughed.

Cole and Seth stopped laughing abruptly. Their sudden nervous expressions put me on alert. I looked at them in confusion. "What?" I asked, re-alizing they weren't watching me, but past me.

As I started to turn my head, Seth said, "You didn't have that talk with Harmony, did you?"

I didn't need to turn all the way around to know she must be here. When I looked behind me, her Jeep was barreling down the dirt drive at a reckless speed. My heart sank. I convinced myself that it would be better to leave without trying to tell her because she'd want answers, and I didn't have any for her.

She skidded to a stop, sending dust clouds into the air. People milling about on the lawn for the estate sale stopped what they were doing to watch. Harmony got out of the car and headed straight for us. I could tell she'd been crying and it ripped my heart out to know that I was responsible.

Seth and Cole quickly headed over to the truck to get out of the line of fire. "Hey Harmony," Cole said nervously as she passed by them.

She ignored him, walking like a woman on a mission. When she reached me she hauled off and slapped me hard across the face. I didn't hold her off or try to defend myself. She didn't stop there. Harmony began to pound my chest with her fists until she had no fight left in her. I took it in silence, which wasn't easy because she was stronger than she looked.

When it appeared she'd gotten the worst of it out of her system, I reached for her. She slapped my arms away and stepped back. I hated to see her hurting like this. "Don't touch me, Liam McKenzie!" she screamed.

She cried, I waited.

Finally, in a broken voice, she asked, "Why?"

"Harmony—"

"Don't say my name. You don't get to say my name." She shook her head. "But you do owe me an explanation." She stood there with her fists clenched and her hair coming out its ponytail. It was all I could do not to hug her to me and beg her forgiveness.

Less than a week ago, I'd plan to marry this woman someday. Now, I was leaving her behind for her own good. Harmony deserved more—not a monster.

"I can't tell you why. It wouldn't make any sense." My voice threatened to break.

"Try me."

I looked into her blue eyes and knew that I'd never see her again. By staying away, I'd be keeping her safe from me and whatever unnatural skeletons were hiding in my past. *That's the way I'd love her.*

"I'm sorry. It's just the way it has to be." I

couldn't look at the pain on her face any longer. I turned to walk toward the truck where Cole and Seth waited.

"I hate you, Liam McKenzie!" she yelled. I heard her get into her Jeep and peel out. I didn't look back. We both knew her words were a lie. It was only a matter of time before the lie became the truth. I'd be okay with that if it stopped her pain and allowed her to move on.

My brothers didn't say a word as I got into the truck. "I love you, Harmony Drake," I whispered, fighting back the tears that I refused to let fall.

Cole got into the other car with Seth. His car was pulling a small trailer with one of the motorcycles the gang left behind. The second one that Cole hid from the authorities mysteriously disappeared the next night.

Nobody claimed the alpha's motorcycle. It was like the spoils of war. Seth decided we might need it and convinced me to bring it with us. I reluctantly agreed. Seth planned to claim it as a salvaged title. We pulled out and drove one last time down the dirt drive to the main road.

Too many heavy thoughts were battling with the excitement of starting a new life. My parents, my birth mother, and the secrets she took with her to the grave, an uncertain future, and Harmony.

I needed to keep my attention on where we were going, not what and who we were leaving behind. *We were headed to Arizona.*

Before we left, we had deliberated over places to live, but Cole's suggestion won over all the other possibilities. He was happy as a lark that we settled on his town. I'd do anything to see that kid smile.

We had one stop on the way to our new life. If we took the 60-south, to the 40-east, we'd be there in two to three days.

But first, we would make a stop in Bowling Green, Kentucky. Seth had been on a mission ever since I'd told him about our birth mother. He'd been searching the internet for tattoo shops and artists, especially the ones who shared their work online.

His theory was that at the time the police were searching for the tattoo artist, many worked off the grid, and their work wasn't as widely shared over social media. It worked. Seth had managed to find an artist who had done a similar tattoo to the one our mother had. They were different, but there were tell-tale signs in the artist's style that were unique to his work.

His name was Terrance Watts and he had a shop in Bowling Green. It would be worth the stop if it gave us any information on our mother.

We found the Dragon's Ink tattoo parlor after only two hours on the road. The shop was in an older part of town. We had to park a few blocks away because of the small trailer we were pulling.

"Cole, you stay with the vehicles. We'll check it out," I said.

"What? Why do I have to stay?" Cole complained.

"Because I'm the oldest and Seth did the work.

Sit tight. We'll only be a minute." He wasn't happy, but he didn't argue anymore as Seth and I headed down the street.

"What do you think we'll find?" Seth asked.

"I'm not sure. A name would help. A lead of some sort." I shoved my hands in my pockets. "I've been wondering if it's such a good idea to know."

Seth looked at me. "I want to know what happened to our birth mother. Don't you think, good or bad, we owe it to her—to ourselves?" he asked.

"I guess."

We reached the door to the shop and entered. A bell above the door chimed and several people looked our way. There were two artists working on customers and several others who looked like they were waiting for their turn or waiting for their friends to finish.

"What can I do for you?" asked a muscular man with long sandy blond hair and sporting intricately tattooed sleeves on both arms. He was bent over a woman who was lying face down on a table. It looked as though he was working on a large tat in the middle of her back.

"We're looking for Terrance Watts," Seth replied.

Everyone stopped whatever they were doing to stare at us. For a long moment, nobody said anything. A nervous tension filled the room. Then the man who had asked put his equipment down wiped his hands on a cloth and bent down to say something to the woman that we couldn't hear.

"I'm not going anywhere," she said.

He stood and motioned for us to follow him through a door in the back. The room through the door looked like a cross between a storage room and an employee lounge. It smelled like weed.

Once we entered, he closed the door, turned and crossed his massive arms over an even more impressive chest. He looked like his five o'clock shadow was a permanent thing.

"What do you want with Terrance?" he asked, eyeing us like we'd done something wrong.

"We just want to talk to him. We have some questions we were hoping he had answers for," I said, keeping my voice friendly.

At first, he just looked between us, like he was trying to figure something out. "Terrance is dead. I'm his brother, Laurence. What were you going to ask him?" This surprised us.

"We're sorry to hear that. When did he pass?" Seth asked.

"Two weeks ago. What's your question?"

Seth and I looked at each other.

"How?" I asked.

"Murdered. Now ask your question before I throw you out of here." He was beginning to look annoyed.

I pulled out the photo of the tattoo on our mother's shoulder and handed it to him. He took it and looked at it closely, then handed it back to me.

"We wanted to know if this was some of your brother's work, or if he knew who did the tattoo," I said, watching his hard face for any sign of recognition.

"It was Terry's. I recognize his work."

I felt a nervous excitement building in my chest. "Do you remember the woman he worked on?" I asked.

"No, but this was an elite brand. Only certain people received this tattoo." He looked hard at us. "I don't know who they were, but I don't think you want to go down that rabbit hole. Terry was afraid of them, whoever they were. He wouldn't even talk to me about them, and we were close. Terry didn't scare easy," he said, walking to the door.

"Please, one last question. Where did he do this tattoo? Was it here?" I asked.

He opened the door. "No, this was when we lived in Tennessee, just outside Nashville. We were street kids back then, working out of our van. Some guy came late one night and said he wanted Terry to make a wolf design for him. Then he had Terry tat about twenty people with the same design. Paid in cash and always in the dead of the night. That's all I know because he always took Terry someplace to do the work." He looked down and shook his head.

"I was always afraid he wouldn't make it back. Fourteen years later, he's killed in a hit and run. Life sucks and then you die."

"You said he was murdered," Seth said.

"Witness said the driver purposely drove onto the curb to hit my brother, then sped off. I trust the person who saw it happen."

We followed him out of the room and thanked him. He walked us to the door. As we left, he said, "As far as anyone is concerned, I didn't tell you anything, right?"

"Hurry up, Laurence. I don't have all day," the woman on the table complained.

We nodded and hurried out.

"That's a great analogy. We're following Alice down the rabbit hole. How can we keep finding more questions than answers?" Seth grumbled as we walked back to the car.

"Maybe we're not meant to know."

"I don't know if I'm okay with that," Seth said as we reached Cole.

"Anything?" Cole asked enthusiastically.

"Just a rabbit hole," I said.

"What?" Cole asked.

"Nothing much. I'll fill you in on the road," Seth said, climbing into his Civic.

"We've got bigger things to worry about." I climbed into the truck and pulled out, knowing Seth would follow.

We had only discussed it a bit, but we were all concerned about shifting and if or when it would happen again. We were heading into the unknown. It was like being thrown into a game where you don't know the rules or the goals. I guess survival is always the goal.

The only certainty we had, was each other. It would be enough—it had to be.

———

Will Liam get another shot at love? Click below to download SPARK and find out.

★★★★★ *"I loved Spark!"*

"A most excellent beginning

to an intriguing series." —
Reader Review

*"First of a new series that I
found very hard to put down."* —
Reader Review

SPARK— **What could be more dangerous to a
secret wolf-shifter than vampires moving into
town? A tenacious news reporter on the hunt
for a story.**

Jessica Parker is beautiful, determined, and
manages to push all of Liam's buttons--good and
bad. She's a skilled reporter and that's the very
reason she's now in danger. Liam's obligated
to keep her at a distance, so she doesn't learn that
he's wilder then she might imagine. Trouble is he's
compelled to protect her because she might be his
true mate. Can he shield her from the vampires,
and still keep his secret safe? Or will he risk it all
and end up on the evening news?

Jessica's hunting a murderer and she knows
that the stern Captain McKenzie is hiding something big. But is the secretive firefighter capable of
murder? If she can keep her wits around him, she
might find out.

*The next three books are full-length novels and
celebrate the Happy-Ever-After we long for.*

Humble request.

Did you enjoy reading ASHES? Please consider leaving a review where ever you buy books and/or Goodreads. Reviews are the single best way for Indie Authors to have their stories discovered by new readers.

Thank you in advance for your support and for reading ASHES.

Turn the page to read an excerpt from Spark, the next book in the Burning Moon Series by RK Close!

Liam

The night is for hunting.

Dried leaves crunch beneath my paws. Small animals scurry to find shelter and crickets chirp their night songs.

The moon bathes the forest in cool shades of blue as it shines brightly amid a starry sky. Frost forms on the ground as the temperature dips below freezing. The cold never concerns me.

I come alive with the sights and sounds of nighttime. A scent catches my attention, excitement quickens my heartbeat. This is what I've been seeking—the hunt is on. I'm more alive in this moment than anytime in my other skin.

My pulse pounds fast and hard in my ears. Four strong legs drive me forward, closer to the prey—our prey. But it is mine first. I am alpha.

Soon, I hear another heartbeat, racing faster than my own. Even the fallen branches and twigs snapping underneath me cannot drown out the panicked thumping of the deer's heart as it desperately tries to flee.

Finally, the moment comes. I leap, making one last contact with a fallen tree that propels me into the air. I collide with the deer, causing the frightened animal to miss a crucial step that sends it crashing to the ground. I'm on it before it can recover. Sharp teeth sink deep into the animal's flesh—my teeth.

Early morning light roused me from a deep sleep

—that, and the sensation of sharp objects poking into my backside. The sun had not risen over the mountains yet, and my breath formed passing clouds with every exhalation. Although my body temperature is hotter than an ordinary human, I shivered. Being naked on the damp forest floor didn't help matters.

Standing, I brushed off the leaves and pine needles that clung to my damp body. Examining the surrounding woods, I searched for my brothers. When I didn't see them, I began the cold walk toward the place we'd stashed our clothing the evening before.

Something about discovering I was a wolf-shifter had the power to free me of the modesty I once possessed. The locals had caught me naked a time or two, but fortunately, none were present today. I always figured I could confess to being a nudist if I had to. While the notion might have been odd, it wouldn't have been unforgivable.

The good people of Flagstaff would accept that concept over the notion of werewolves living among them, especially with our proximity to the neighboring town of Sedona. Now that there was an interesting place. Sedona, home to nudists, spiritualists, and a few self-proclaimed witches—among other crazy ideas.

I heard my brother's footsteps as dry pine needles and twigs crunched beneath his bare feet long before I saw him emerge from the forest. Heightened strength, speed, smell, and hearing were just a few benefits of being a shifter.

Seth fell into step beside me, and we walked in

silence, attempting to shake off the deep sleep that follows shifting from one form to another. I glanced sideways at my younger brother, and he graced me with one of his devil-may-care grins. Seth was only an inch shorter than me—making him six foot, two inches and one hundred ninety pounds of trouble. His jet-black hair hung just long enough to raise questions, but not long enough to get him written up at work.

We reached the small cave. It wasn't large enough to crawl deeper than four feet inside. Seth pulled out three bundles of clothing and personal items. The freezing temperature was an excellent motivation for dressing quickly. If I'd been merely human, I'd have been suffering from hypothermia already.

I stepped into my jeans and slid my arms into a flannel shirt before sitting down to put my hiking boots on. Seth still hadn't bothered to button his shirt or zip his pants. Instead, he busied himself with checking his phone, as if it weren't freezing.

Only a few minutes had passed before Cole came running toward us in all his naked glory. Our youngest brother always had a ton of energy and struggled with slow and easy. His grim expression alerted me that his hurried pace wasn't simply his usual enthusiasm for life. Something was wrong.

"We got trouble," Cole said when he arrived. He took the pile of clothes Seth handed him and dressed quickly.

"What's up?" Seth asked. I scanned the forest —alert to signs of danger.

Cole was shorter and stockier than Seth or myself, but his sandy blond hair matched mine.

He wore it short on the sides but longer on top. When he was younger, it used to hang over his eyes, and he was forever combing it back with his fingers.

"I stumbled across two campers—dead—about a mile up the trail." Cole looked shaken up. Finding dead people could do that to a person. But he was also a firefighter and EMT, like Seth and me, so he didn't rattle easily.

"Did you . . . ?" Seth asked.

Cole stared at him in confusion until he realized what Seth was implying. Then he looked indignant. "No! Of course not. It wasn't me. Don't blame the messenger."

Seth and I exchanged a glance. We knew that we retained only flashes of memory while in wolf form. It was the fear of hurting someone that sent us far into the mountains when we needed to shift. It was an itch that had to be scratched. I'd taken a life once, but I tried not to dwell on that if I could help it.

"Don't shoot the messenger," Seth corrected.

Cole shrugged his shoulders. He finished putting on his shoes and was soon leading us to the bodies.

"How'd they die?" I asked as we walked.

"I can't be sure. I only checked for a pulse, even though I knew they were gone. Figured since I'm a firefighter, the police would wonder why I hadn't followed procedure. There's something else odd about it." Cole glanced sideways at me.

"What?" I asked.

"You should see for yourself—or smell," Cole mumbled before turning his attention ahead. He didn't speak again until we saw a red tent in the distance. "That's it."

We were a hundred yards away from the campsite, but that was close enough for me to understand what Cole was talking about. There was the stink of death, but not only that. There was something more.

"What the hell is that?" I asked as we drew closer.

"It's not that bad," Seth said. "Nothing I've ever smelled before, though."

Cole and I stopped to gawk at Seth. "Not that bad?" Cole demanded. "That odor is just wrong."

"It's different, that's all. What are you girls getting your panties in a wad over?" Seth asked.

I had a bad feeling about the lingering scent, but I kept it to myself. We reached the edge of the camp, and I took in the scene before me. A small table sat on its side, and several items lay strewn across the ground. The tent seemed to have avoided damage.

"Did you check for anyone else?" I asked.

"Yes, I used a stick to pull the flap back, and I also searched the perimeter. Nothing."

I nodded and walked carefully to the first body. It was a young woman, mid-to-late twenties, with long brown hair. She wore a blue down coat, and a beanie of the same color was lying a few feet away. Her eyes stared blankly at the morning sky while her hair fanned out around her, a few strands across her pale face.

"Look at her neck," Cole said.

I carefully moved the strands of hair away. Bruising and a small amount of dried blood dotted her neck—along with two puncture wounds. The front of her jacket looked as though something had sliced it up, but there were no obvious injuries in relation. Possibly someone grabbed her by the coat. The location of the tears would support that theory, but who had the strength to go through nylon like that?

"What could that smell be, Liam?" Cole asked.

I glanced at the male a few feet away. By the angle of his arm, it had been broken before he died. He also had a wound on his throat, but the damage was more extensive than on the woman. If I had to guess, I'd put their deaths at six or seven hours ago. It bothered me that this had happened in the same proximity as my brothers and me. Something other than us was hunting last night.

The Coconino National Forest was 1.8 million acres of territory. This particular patch of woods was ours. We chose it because of its remote location and the fact that people rarely used this part of the mountain range. These unlucky folks were off the grid, but occasionally people wanted to be away from it all.

I spotted a book of matches next to the tent and bent to pick it up. After dusting it off, I handed it to Seth. He turned it over in his fingers, and then passed it to Cole.

"The Burning Moon Bar," Cole read, then

looked up at me. "They must have been in town at some point. Look at their gear. Too much to be backpacking. They carried it in from a car. That means they parked near your truck, Liam."

"They arrived after we did." Seth gave me a worried glance. "We should walk away, right?"

I shook my head. "I don't think we can. We were roaming all over these woods last night. If we don't report this, we could find the finger pointing at us. Whoever or whatever did this isn't a shifter, but they aren't human either. The safest thing to do is report it. I'll say that we came across the bodies and then hiked back to the truck for better cell service."

I looked at them, and they nodded. This wasn't the situation I'd planned for, but it was the reason I kept our camping gear in my truck. We needed to support the well-known belief that we camped together often.

I held out my hand, and Cole passed me the matchbook case, which I slipped into my pocket before heading for the parking lot. Cole and Seth followed.

Ordinarily, we'd be laughing and cutting up by now. This morning was somber and gray— matching our moods. We were silent out of respect for the two people whose lives were cut short.

When we reached the clearing that passed for a trailhead parking lot, there was a small blue car. Two paper hearts hung from the rearview mirror. The vehicle had California plates, which most likely meant they were tourists passing through or college students attending Northern Arizona University.

I made the call that would bring the sheriff and open a can of worms I wished we could avoid. Whatever did this, I hoped it had already left town, even if I was curious about what other supernatural beings existed, besides shifters like us. Not that we needed any mysteries to solve. Our own past was full of unanswered questions.

End of sample. Continue reading Spark now!

VAMPIRE FILES

RED NIGHT EXCERPT

Dirty little secrets are my bread and butter. Everyone has them, or I would be broke. Most people are born with some talents; musical, lovely singing voice, athletic, good with numbers or an eye for design. I'm not good at any of those things, but I am a professional people-watcher. I like to study them, unravel their mysteries. Reading people is like a hobby or maybe a life skill that turned into a career.

In a matter of moments, I have most people figured out. Ninety percent of the time, my sixth sense is spot on. I read people like someone might read a book—part feeling, part observation. My mom called it, my gift—typical mom response.

The instrumental version of *Grandma Got Ran*

Over by a Reindeer plays in the background. Busy shoppers move past me as if they're running out of time. With the extended holiday hours at the Scottsdale Fashion Mall, they're feeding their retail addiction late into the evening. Thanksgiving hasn't even passed, yet Christmas sales and shopping have begun in full force. I'm not here for sales, but I am interested in a certain female shopper.

Reading people is easy—too easy, like knowing the ending of the story by the first chapter. Money, sex, and power are prime motivating factors—at least for the people I'm hired to expose.

The coffee in my cup is cold, but I still toy with the paper cup for something to do. When my stomach rumbles loudly, I'm reminded that I missed dinner. I hope nobody noticed. After adjusting myself, and my stomach, into a different position, I return my focus to the Tiffany & Co. store across the mall. Just in time, I notice a tall attractive woman with long auburn hair walking out of the store with a man that I don't recognize.

The woman, Rebecca Tanner, is on the arm of a dark-haired man wearing a gray tailored suit. Both look as though they belong on the cover of a magazine instead of shopping at the local mall. They do make a striking pair.

Rebecca's a beautiful woman, and she knows it. The man has movie star quality written all over him. He stands out like a sore thumb.

Rebecca smiles and leans into him. Her eyes never leave him—making her look like an adoring fan. On the other hand, the man appears preoccupied as he leads Jessica swiftly through the crowd. She's my target tonight, but he's the surprise.

Where did you come from, Mystery Man?

Tossing my coffee in the trash, I throw my messenger bag over my shoulder and begin to follow them. Keeping a low profile is the key to stalking someone. It's difficult to spy on people once they've noticed you, even once.

Mystery Man's dark hair catches the light and gives him an unearthly glow. If he's hanging out with Rebecca, he's no angel. I appreciate his broad shoulders that taper down to a slim waist. Even the expensive suit can't hide his long muscular legs.

There's an air of confidence in the way he holds himself that causes shoppers to quickly part around him—many stopping to stare or catch a second look. Most likely, they're trying to remember if he's a celebrity they should know.

Nobody moves for me, so I'm forced to dodge bodies as I try to keep pace with them. This evening may have developed an interesting twist, a bump in the road. I love bumps and twists. They make life, and especially work, more interesting. Part of the problem with the sixth sense thing— I'm not easily surprised.

The couple turns down a long hallway that leads to the public restrooms, but they continue on until they reach double metal doors marked EMPLOYEES ONLY. Mystery Man looks over his shoulder before pushing through the doors. I quickly stop to study a poster for—men's underwear. Nice.

Hmmm.

Without slowing my pace, I pull my long hair into a quick, messy bun. Before I reach the doors, I've pulled a solid black apron from my bag and slip it over my head—never missing a beat. This apron is the best ten dollars I've ever spent. It gets me into all sorts of places. Add a fake name tag, and I'm unstoppable.

Thankfully I'm wearing sneakers tonight.

On the other side of the doors, I find a dimly lit industrial-looking hall with more gray metal doors. There's a stark difference between the bright lights and holiday music of the mall to the colorless atmosphere of the corridor.

Moving purely on instinct, I head left down the hall and around a corner. I find a door marked EXIT. Not knowing what's on the other side, I stop to compose myself and push stray strands of hair from my face. Easing the door open, I feel a burst of cool air.

I peer into a dark concrete jungle—also known as the underground parking garage. My car is down here, but I couldn't say where. The mall is enormous.

Lighting in the garage is almost nonexistent, which makes the dim hallway I'd just left behind seem inviting. I notice a couple of fluorescent lights are out, while another one flickers as if it's only a matter of time. A dark abyss greets me in either direction. Gone are the bustling shoppers for the moment. The eerie silence is a sobering reminder that I've left safety far behind.

A noise, a slight scraping sound, to my left

draws my attention. It may have come from the corner where the light refuses to touch. Narrowing my eyes, I try to focus all of my senses on the blackness. I look away when I'm unable to make out more than inky shadows.

They couldn't have left, so, where are they?

I consider pulling out my small flashlight to shine into car windows when I hear it again—the same scraping sound coming from that same corner. *Gotcha.*

Even though I can't see them, they could be watching me. Just in case, I casually walk in the opposite direction until I turn a corner. Crouching low behind a row of cars and begin working my way back to them.

At times like this, I wish my legs weren't so long. My thighs burn as I duck-walk my way closer. I'm also wishing yesterday wasn't leg day at the gym.

I situate myself behind a dark sedan that's roughly sixty feet away from where I believe they are. As my eyes finally begin to adjust to the lighting conditions, forms solidify and become more recognizable. Rebecca Tanner is one busy gal. Having an affair with my client's husband must not be enough to entertain her. We can add hooking up with random strangers at the mall to her resume. Assuming they are strangers.

Maybe he's an old flame and they just happened to bump into each other. Either way, she's cheating on the cheater—that's poetic justice at its finest.

There was a time earlier in my career when

spying on unsuspecting individuals caused me to suffer major loads of guilt. It's like digging around in people's dirty laundry. Eventually, my skin got thicker, and my sensibilities became... less sensitive.

I don't make people cheat on their spouse or steal from their employers. I simply make good money when they do. Some people may be tempted to label me a voyeur. I know I'm not. Finding answers to questions and giving people closure is incredibly satisfying.

As quietly as possible, I slip my camera, with a telephoto lens, from my bag and set the aperture to pull as much light as possible, without using the flash. I've got one goal at this point—get some shots, then get the heck out of Dodge before the love-birds take it to the next level. I raise the camera to my eye, begin to focus, and pause.

What I initially perceived as a passionate embrace suddenly looks suspicious. Mystery Man has a hand intertwined in her long hair, while his face is buried in her neck. His other hand has a death grip on her arm.

If he keeps that up, there's going to be a mark. Rebecca will be wearing long sleeves and turtlenecks for weeks. Hollywood visions of vampires fill my head. I clamp a hand over my mouth in order to hold off manic laughter that threatens to bubble up.

Those movies have never been my thing, but I've watched a few. I prefer comedies. Pop culture likes its romance with a touch of horror and vio-

lence mixed in. I've never understood the at-
traction.

After my humor is under control, my stomach
still feels uneasy. Then the hairs on the back of my
neck stand on end. It's not like me to let my imagi-
nation run away. I am a professional, after all.
Maybe it's low blood sugar that's making me feel
goofy.

I can't fight the nagging feeling that I'm wit-
nessing a crime. I'm simply not sure what crime
that would be. *Death by hickey?*

I was hired to prove that my client's husband is
having an affair with another woman. He is, and
Rebecca Tanner is the other woman. Her husband
stands to lose his marriage of twenty-four years
and a great deal of his wealth because of his relationship with Ms. Tanner.

How I would love to be a fly on the wall when
the lawyer presents him with these photos. Re-
venge won't mend my client's broken heart, but it
might help that bitter pill to go down easier.

Nights like these, I feel like an avenging angel
—*minus the wings.*

It may not be angelic making a living exposing
cheaters, liars, and thieves. But, the money is
good, I set my own schedule and enjoy most of the
challenges that my career presents; like how to get
out of here before clothing items start to fly and
my photos become pornographic.

Click!

The moment that I press the button to take the
first of many incriminating pictures, Mystery

Man's head rises a fraction as his eyes lock with mine. My heart may have skipped a beat or two.

Holy, crap!

He could not have heard that. But there he is, looking right at me. I've never felt so naked or exposed.

With his lips still on Rebecca's neck, his gaze never leaves me. A sheen of perspiration coats my skin as panic rises in my chest. Neither of us moves for what feels like an eternity. Even without help from the telephoto lens, I can clearly see his eyes in the darkness. Some trick of the light causes them to glow.

Without releasing his gaze, I blindly shove my camera in my bag as I prepare to make a run for it. I only look away the moment I'm ready to bolt.

Murphy's Law is in full force when my foot catches on the apron. I stumble, landing hard on my hands and knees. My hair, having come loose from the hastily styled bun, now hangs over my face like a curtain. Frantically, I shove my hair out of my way with my free hand.

Too late. He's reached me first. Somehow, Mystery Man has breached the distance between us and stands a mere car's length away, looking down at me like I'm his worst enemy.

A quick assessment tells me that my defense skills will only prolong the inevitable. His eyes are a serious distraction. They're the bluest I've ever seen. But, it's the murderous look in them that promises it's about to get ugly.

Did he growl at me? I think he did.

When he begins to move toward me with lethal

grace, I'm reminded of a panther moving in for the kill. Under any other circumstances, I'd admire someone his size maneuvering this easily, like a dancer who has performed the steps a thousand times.

Does Death dance? I think I'm about to find out.

Like a deer in the headlights, I freeze. So much for my years of self-defense training—it just flew out the window. My limbs refused to move, and my throat feels like I've been days without water. A slave to fear, my traitorous body refuses to obey my mental commands. I can't even manage a scream.

He's like a predator, sensing my fear and reacting to it. Just as he's about to touch me, several young men burst from the stairwell, laughing and talking loudly. Mystery Man stops, his hand only inches from me. Slowly, reluctantly he pulls his gaze from mine to glare in the direction of the group of men.

The moment he looks away something in me clicks, and I immediately move into action. My body feels awkward at first, as though I'm moving through water. I scramble backward. Finding my missing voice, I yell at the men, even as I stand and begin running toward them. "Hey, over here!" My voice sounds raspy and hoarse.

My unsuspecting rescuers look startled but alert. They glance past me, searching for a threat. Their expressions register concern but not the reaction I'm expecting. Confused, I spin around only to find Mystery Man and Rebecca have disappeared.

I turn around in a circle, but it's as if they've vanished into thin air.

He's gone. That should make me feel safe, but for some reason, it doesn't.

Start the Vampire Files Trilogy tonight! Go to www.RKCloseBooks.com to learn more.

For my Kentucky family...

Our roots are deep.

ACKNOWLEDGMENTS

Thank you;

To my editor for this book, Toni Rakestraw, for her patience and enthusiasm for my writing. I'm not the easiest writer to work with, especially when I don't follow the rules.

My fellow authors who share their vast knowledge so willingly. There are too many to list, but you know who you are. Elicia, Juliet, Leila, Nicole, Rebecca…

I'd like to mention Author, Liz Durando for always having an answer for my endless questions and for being so ready to share her wealth of knowledge with others.

For friends who support me in so many ways, like reading my books, even though urban fantasy isn't their cup of tea.

And, the family who've cheered me on and the few that have become fans. I always acknowledge my husband Greg and our kids, who occasionally sacrifice time, meals, clean clothing, and more to allow me to spin my stories and chase my dreams.

My greatest thanks goes to you, my readers. Without you, it's only words on a page.

RK Close

ABOUT THE AUTHOR

Best-selling author RK Close blends urban fantasy and paranormal romantic suspense into fast-paced, hard-to-put-down, adventures that keep fans on the edge of their seats and coming back for more.

An outdoor enthusiast, nomadic traveler, wife, mother and lover of all things curry, RK spends her spare time with her head in a book, behind a camera, canvas, hiking, traveling, or walking her three high-maintenance dogs. Her book addiction began in high school and bloomed into a writing career later in life.

Never miss a new release or giveaway from this author. Subscribe to RK Close's newsletter today!

RK Close Newsletter

COPYRIGHT

BURNING MOON SERIES

Made in the USA
Las Vegas, NV
15 March 2024